MAYBE NEVER

MAYBE, DEFINITELY BOOK 2

ELLA MILES

FREE BOOKS

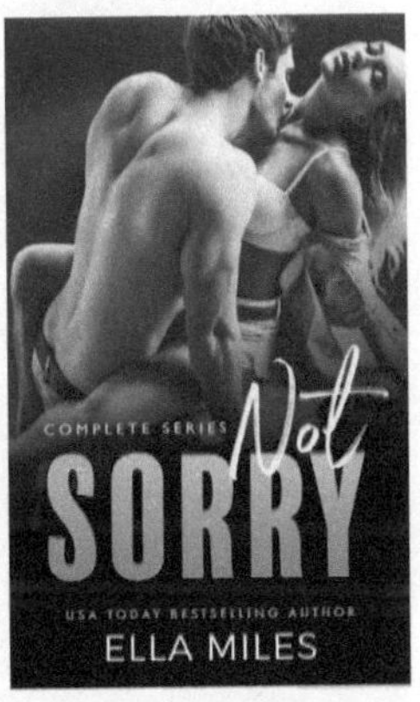

Read **Not Sorry** for **FREE**! And sign up to get my latest releases, updates, and more goodies here→EllaMiles.com/freebooks

Follow me on BookBub to get notified of my new releases and recommendations here→Follow on BookBub Here

Join Ella's Bellas FB group for giveaways and FUN→Join Ella's Bellas Here

Will one mistake destroy her life? Will one secret? One lie?

Kinsley Felton thought she had found a solution to her problems. She thought she had convinced her family that she is strong enough to run the company, if not on her own, then with help. She thought she had won when she decided not to marry Killian and instead just date him. But everything she thought was wrong.

Killian isn't who she thought he was. Now she is sitting in a jail cell for something she didn't do because of him. But maybe she deserves to sit in jail anyway to pay for her past mistakes. All she knows is she needs to stay far away from Killian no matter how much her heart aches for him.

Will Kinsley let herself get lost in the deceit or will she save herself and take another chance at love?

MAYBE, DEFINITELY SERIES:

Maybe Yes
Maybe Never
Maybe Always

Definitely Yes
Definitely No
Definitely Forever

KINSLEY

I PACE back and forth in the holding cell, unable to sit patiently like the rest of my cellmates. One woman lies back on one of the benches, seemingly asleep, while another sits across from her, picking the nail polish off her fingers.

Not me though. I can't sit. Not when I have no idea why I'm here. So, instead, I pace back and forth in the small cell, hoping that, soon, someone will come to tell me what the hell is going on. I also have to pee, which is keeping me from sitting down, but I'm not going to go in the toilet in the corner of the room—at least not until I can't hold it any longer.

I think back to the last time I was here. It was the same jail and the same holding cell with the same disgusting yellow walls. Last time, I was calmer, much calmer, because I had accepted that I deserved to be in prison. I had confessed.

I stop pacing when the woman lying on the bench snores, startling me. I don't know why I'm back in jail now. *What did I do?* The agent mentioned something about fraud and money laundering. I didn't do either of those things. It must be a mistake.

And Killian...

I can barely even let my heart go there. One day—actually, less than a day, more like one hour, was all I got with Killian. It's all the time I got to think about a possible future with him.

I thought I loved him.

I thought he was the one for me.

I was wrong.

Killian isn't Killian. Killian is a liar. I chose wrong, again.

I glance at the clock barely visible outside the holding cell. It's past midnight. They won't question me tonight. I won't be arraigned tonight. They won't do anything with me tonight. I'm stuck here, in this cold room, with two strange women.

I take a seat on the only remaining bench in the room and rest my head against the wall. I cross my arms over my chest and rub my hands over them, trying to warm up, but I'm still shivering. I push the urge to pee, along with thoughts of why I'm in here, out of my head. I push Killian out of my head until the only thing that remains is last time.

This feels just like last time when I had fallen for a man who wasn't what he seemed. Now, I fell again for the wrong man. Even though my father and grandfather had handpicked him, they picked wrong. Maybe there isn't a man out there for me.

I should have learned my lesson the first time. Instead, I'm back in this cell again, and this time, I don't know when I'll be getting out.

2

______

KINSLEY

FIVE YEARS EARLIER

THE BELL RINGS, and I walk from my English class to my locker. I feel the excitement floating off the students and teachers all around me, as everyone is happy to be ending another school year. Everyone is excited, except me.

I walk slowly through the hallway, hoping to get one last glimpse of the man I'm crazy about. One last glance of the man whom I will probably never see again. That's not true. I'll occasionally see him at family functions that involve close family friends, just like I always have. But it won't be the same as seeing him every day in the hallway, at lunch, or on the football field every fall.

The man I'm in love with is graduating today and is going to UCLA in the fall while I'll be stuck here, in Las Vegas, for another year. I could follow him to UCLA when I graduate, but there's a high chance that, by then, he'll already have a girlfriend and have forgotten all about me.

I stop at my locker, pausing for far longer than it takes for me to get my backpack out so I can look for him. His locker is just across the hallway from mine, but he never comes.

In frustration, I slam my locker door closed and begin the long walk to my car. I continue to walk slowly, hoping to see him if I stall long enough. I don't though. I don't seem him anywhere.

I get to my white Lexus faster than I had hoped. I open the door and slam it in frustration because I didn't see him. I didn't get to say good-bye one last time. I don't get to hear his voice one final time. He didn't care enough to find me.

I shake my head as I start up the engine. *Why should he care about coming to see me?* I'm nobody to him. Just a lowly sophomore who has been friends with his family since forever. Just a stupid girl who has a silly crush on him, just like every other girl in the school whom he doesn't care about. And he sure as hell doesn't love me.

I'm tired of being that girl though—the girl who is a goody-two-shoes, who gets good grades, and who follows the social hierarchy. I want to go after the bad boy who everyone wants but is too afraid to go after.

I'm going after the man I love. I'm going after the bad boy. I'm going after Tristan Slade.

I grab the door handle to go find him, but a tap at my window startles me, and I stop short. I turn to see who it is, assuming it's Eli since he asked me out earlier this week, and I have yet to give him an answer. I couldn't, not when there was still a chance that Tristan might want to date me.

I should say yes though. Eli is a good person, attractive, and smart. My family has known his family for years as well. I should say yes to him.

It's not Eli at my window though. It's Tristan. And he has a wicked grin on his face as he flips his long brown hair out of his eyes. I roll down my window as my breath quickens, like it always does every time he comes near me.

I open my mouth to ask what he's doing here, but no words come out. I feel my face burn in embarrassment.

He smiles bigger. "You didn't think I'd leave without telling my favorite girl good-bye, did ya?"

I smile and take a deep breath. "No."

Tristan leans into the car, giving me a quick hug and peck on the cheek. My body immediately relaxes. That was all I wanted—a chance to feel just for a moment that he cares about me even if he only thinks about me as an annoying little sister.

He pulls his head back out of the window, and I think he's going to go. I'm surprised his entourage hasn't found him yet to drag him back to wherever the latest party is. He pauses for a second as he stands outside my car, looking at me.

"You want to go to a party with me tonight?"

I raise my eyebrows at him. He didn't really say that. He didn't just ask me out. It must be an illusion. So, I just smile innocently at him and pretend normal words just came out of his mouth instead of the ludicrous words I heard.

He reaches his hand into the car until he's touching my cheek. "Kinsley, are you okay?"

I swallow down the lump that has made its way up my throat. "Yes."

"Your cheeks just look even redder than usual."

He removes his hand from my cheek, and my hand replaces it. My cheek does feel warmer than usual, probably because it liked the way his hand caressed it.

"So, I'll pick you up at seven then, Kins?"

I nod although I'm not sure what I'm nodding to. He smiles and winks at me before he walks away, leaving me alone in my car. Leaving me alone to realize that Tristan Slade just asked me out.

I've changed a hundred times since I got home from school. I don't know what to wear. Tristan never said what party we were going to, although I can guess. Only a handful of people would be lucky enough to host a party Tristan Slade would attend. Vanessa, Cade, or Samantha are at the top of my list.

I hear the doorbell ring downstairs, and every nerve in my body ignites with anxiety. It's just after seven. It's him. I know it without glancing out the window to see if his black Mustang convertible is here. I know.

I grab my red jacket and slip it on over my white crop top I've paired with a short black skirt and heels. I zip up the jacket so my father won't be able to see my bare stomach before I go out.

I haven't gone out on a date before, and although I've modeled similar outfits in magazines, I have no idea how he would respond to me wearing something like this on a date. And I'm not going to press my luck and embarrass myself by having my father force me to change my clothes when he sees a boy is coming to pick me up—especially a boy like Tristan. Even though my father has known him since we were both toddlers, it doesn't mean my father likes or trusts him.

I walk down the stairs and find Tristan standing in the entryway, smiling at me. I pause as my heart skips at his smile before I check out the rest of his body. He's wearing jeans, a dark shirt, and a leather jacket, despite the warm weather outside.

"You look beautiful. You ready to go?"

I hold up a finger, indicating I need one second. I skip past Tristan to let my father know I'm going out. I check his office, but he isn't in there. He never is. I try the kitchen next and find him making himself a peanut butter sandwich—the only thing he knows how to make for himself.

He looks me up and down. "Going somewhere?"

"Just out to some graduation parties."

He smiles and nods. "With a Mr. Tristan Slade."

My eyes widen. "How did you…"

He shakes his head and puts the top piece of bread onto his sandwich. "I was at his father's house the other week. The topic of you two together got brought up."

My mouth drops. *They were talking about the two of us? Is Tristan only going out with me because of my father and his father's relationship?*

"You're okay with me going out tonight?" I ask.

My father walks over and softly kisses me on the forehead. "You look beautiful, princess. Of course I'm okay with you going out tonight, even if I'm not thrilled with the idea of you dating yet."

I smile brightly at him. "I'll be back by curfew." I turn to leave.

"Stay out as long as you want."

I turn back to see my father casually walking back to his sandwich. "You deserve to have a bit of fun for once in your life. Just don't tell your mother." He winks at me.

I take a deep breath, feeling better about tonight now I know it can last as long as I want, which is forever if I get my way.

I turn to walk back to Tristan, but I still hear my father's words as I leave.

"I'm sorry, princess."

I pause for just a second at his words. *Why would he say he's sorry when he just said I could go out?* I turn back to ask him, but he's gone, and Tristan is waiting.

I find Tristan still standing in the entryway.

"Ready," I say, unzipping my jacket a little as I approach him.

He smiles at me and grabs ahold of my hand when I get close. I freeze at his sudden touch. We've touched before, but we've never held hands, not like this. This touch, I love.

We walk to his car, hand in hand. He only lets go after he has opened the door, and I have to climb in. I unzip my jacket and take it off as he climbs into the driver's side. He starts the car and backs it down the driveway.

Grab my hand, I think.

I rest my hand on my thigh for easy access, but he doesn't grab it. And I'm not bold enough to grab his—at least not yet, but maybe by the end of the night.

"Where are we going?" I ask in a shaky voice.

"Vanessa Waters' party. We just need to make a quick stop first to pick something up."

I nod, not surprised by his choice of party. I don't ask where we are going first though because I assume it's to pick up alcohol or something for the party. I just hope it's not to pick up another girl.

"How does it feel to be done with school?" I ask, trying to keep my mind off the fact we could be on our way to pick up another girl.

"It feels awesome as fuck." He winks at me.

I tuck my curly, long blonde hair behind my ear. I don't know what else to say to Tristan. I don't know what else to do. This is going to be a long night if I don't think of more to say—and soon.

So, I say the only other thing that's on my mind, "My father said he talked to your dad this past week about us. Do you know what that was about?"

Tristan keeps his eyes on the road. "No, I don't talk to my father much."

I look down at my hands in my lap. "You didn't ask me out because one of our fathers asked you to. Did you?"

He glances my way now with a deep frown on his face. It is quickly replaced with a smile as he grabs my hand and pulls it to his lips, softly kissing the back of my hand.

"You're here because I like you."

My heart flutters at the thought. *Tristan likes me.*

———

Tristan holds my hand as we walk down the strip toward the Felton Grand.

When he parked just off the strip, I curiously looked at him, but I didn't have the courage to ask him why we were here. I don't know what we are doing here, and I'm more nervous than ever Tristan is only going out with me because of my father or his.

"What are we doing here?" I finally get the courage to ask as we enter the casino my father owns.

He smiles at me just as confidently as before. "I have to pick up a package, and then we will head over to the party."

I take a deep breath as we walk onto the casino floor. I'm going to be noticed by someone here. I spend almost every day after school here with my father. Everyone knows who I am. I don't want them to notice. I don't want to feel embarrassed because I am here with a guy.

"What kind of package?" I ask.

His eyes scan the floor, looking for whomever we are meeting. And then his eyes see my worried face, and his smile turns to a frown. "What's wrong, Kinsley?"

"I-I don't want anyone to know we are here." I tug on my

long curls, twirling them in my hand, to try to keep my nerves at bay. I let my eyes just barely meet his. "I don't understand what we are doing here. I just want to go to the party."

Tristan's frown relaxes. He tightens his grip on my hand and walks me back to the lobby. I follow, glad to leave the casino floor without being spotted and questioned, but I now feel like a scared little girl. That's not how I want to seem to him.

He lets go of my hand. "I'll be right back," he says, distracted by his mission, until he sees my face.

Whatever he sees makes him pause before walking the foot back to me. He tucks a loose strand of hair behind my ear before leaning toward me.

I watch his lips lower, and smile, expecting to feel a kiss on my cheek. Instead, his lips land on my lips. I suck in a breath when I feel his moist lips touch mine. He quickly slips his tongue into my mouth and tangles his hand in my hair, not settling on just a quick peck on the lips.

I've had only one other kiss on the lips. I was twelve, and the boy kissed me on a dare. It was nothing like this. This is a real kiss. This is what being kissed by Tristan Slade feels like. It feels magical, feeling his lips on mine. I feel important. I feel special. And, for the first time, I feel *wanted*.

When his lips leave mine, a smile curls on my lips. I don't open my eyes, but I can feel him grinning at my smile.

"I'll be right back," he says.

I nod and keep my eyes closed. I let my whole body take in every feeling from that kiss and lock it away in my memory forever. I don't want to forget it. Not even after I go on more dates and date more men. Not after I'm married with kids. Not when I'm ninety. I don't want to ever forget how I feel right now because I can't imagine anything feeling better.

I open my eyes when I'm sure the memory is forever ingrained in my head. I don't let my mind drift back to whatever silly reason we are here instead of already at Vanessa's party right now. All I can think about is that Tristan likes me.

I keep my eyes glued on the hallway that leads to the casino floor as it tempts me to go find him. My previous worries of being spotted by someone who knows me left the moment his lips touched mine. Now, all I care about is being close to him.

I take a couple of steps forward, unable to wait any longer in the lobby where he left me, when I see him rounding the corner. It doesn't keep me from moving closer to him though. I stop when I'm a foot away from him, realizing I don't know what to do. I want to kiss him again, but a second kiss now would be too soon after the first. I want to hold his hand again.

I can do that, I think.

Then, I see the small black bag in his hand. My eyelids blink rapidly as I try to understand what I'm seeing, but I don't understand what is in the bag. It's not alcohol. It almost looks like it could be...

Tristan tucks the bag into his jacket pocket when he notices my stare, and he quickly takes my hand back in his. My thoughts of what could be in the bag drift away. I longingly look up at him, but he just smiles at me. I guess I won't be getting my second kiss after all.

———

The music is loud and overwhelming as we enter Vanessa's

parents' house. I lose Tristan's hand as we enter the house, immediately making me feel cold and empty. He keeps walking toward a group of seniors in the living room while I stand frozen in the entryway crowded with people. Everyone has a red Solo cup in their hand and a smile on their face. Everyone is happy to be at the last party of the year and to have a break from school for the summer.

I haven't been to many parties like this—not that I haven't been invited because I have. I have just always been the good girl, the rule-follower. I never felt the need to go to parties with underage drinking and who-knows-what going on upstairs, but all it took was Tristan asking me out, and now here I am.

I walk into the living room where Tristan is, but I feel a hand on my shoulder immediately bringing me to a halt. The hand isn't Tristan's. I know that because I can see him across the room, laughing at something Vanessa said. She's whom he should be with, not me. She's beautiful, confident, and a bit of a rebel, just like him. She's nothing like me.

I turn to see whose hand is on my shoulder, and I find Eli standing there, smiling brightly at me.

"I didn't know you would be at this party."

I force my lips to return his smile. "I didn't know I would be here either."

"Let me get you a drink," he says.

"No need," Tristan says, thrusting a red cup of beer into my hand.

I smile at him and take the cup. "I'll see you later," I say to Eli.

Tristan guides me away from Eli. He stops and raises his eyebrow at me. "You and Eli?"

"No," I say quickly.

"Good," he says, wrapping his arm around my waist like he owns me.

I take a sip of the beer. It's warm and disgusting, but I force the liquid down my throat anyway. And then I take another sip and another.

Tristan guides me outside to the back of the house where there is a DJ and a makeshift dance floor set up next to the pool. Several people are already in the pool in various stages of dress—fully clothed or just underwear. And I saw one guy who was either naked or wearing nude-colored underwear.

"Want to dance?"

"I'd love to." I feel my face light up brightly.

I watch as Tristan downs his beer, and I do the same. He takes my cup from me and tosses our cups on the floor. He then takes my hand and moves me onto the crowded dance floor.

We begin dancing effortlessly to the music. We're not touching, despite how badly I want to touch him, but then, as if God were answering my prayers, I'm bumped forward into Tristan's arms. I giggle up at him, embarrassed that my hands are now pressed against his firm chest. He doesn't seem to mind though. Instead, he twirls me around so my back is pressed against his chest and my ass is pressed firmly against him. His arms wrap tightly around me, and we begin dancing again.

How could this get any better?

That's when I feel his hot breath against my ear.

"You're a good dancer."

I feel my cheeks flush. "You, too."

His lips touch a place I've never been touched before— my neck. I never imagined that place would feel so good, and it causes me to moan at the unexpected pleasure. My soft moan only encourages him further.

I glance around the dance floor as his kisses travel lower to my shoulder. I'm worried someone is going to see us, but no one is watching.

He spins me back around, still holding me in his arms, and his typical wicked grin is on his face. This time, when he leans in, I expect him to kiss me on the lips, not the cheek. I meet him halfway until our lips are pressed together.

I surprise myself by slipping my tongue into his mouth before he has the chance to do it to me. My hands automatically go around his neck as I lose myself in the kiss. His hands find my hips, holding me tightly against him, until I think I can feel his erection growing against me—an erection I am causing with my kiss.

When he pulls away, just an inch from my lips, I'm panting hard. The kiss has stolen most of my breath from me.

He glances up at the house and then back at me. "Let's go."

I narrow my eyes. *Go? We just got here.*

Tristan grabs my hand, and then he's guiding me through the crowd of people and back into the house. I follow because I want to be with him, but I feel like I did something wrong if he already wants to go.

We walk back through the living room, and several guys he was talking to earlier wink at him as we walk by. I just smile at them, like I know what they are doing, but I don't. I don't know why they winked at Tristan.

We walk back to the entryway, and I expect him to lead us out of the house. He doesn't. Instead, he leads me up the stairs of the house, up to where there are fewer people.

We pass closed door after closed door until he sees a door cracked open. Tristan peeks his head in and gives one look to someone inside the room. A young boy, who I'm guessing is closer to my age than Tristan's, scurries out with who I assume is his date behind him.

Tristan leads me into the room and immediately makes his intentions clear. He slams the door behind us and presses my back against it. His lips attack mine in a kiss that is more carnal and passionate than any kiss I've had before.

I smile and kiss him back. I was wrong. This kiss is better than the first kiss he gave me in the lobby of my father's casino. This is the kiss I need to remember.

This kiss doesn't stop though. It continues right into the next and then the next.

His hands travel over my stomach and to the bottom of my shirt. I suck in a breath but don't stop him as his hand slides under my shirt. I break from his lips when his hand fondles my breast. It's too much pleasure to feel both his kiss and his touch at the same time.

He doesn't allow me much of a break before his lips find mine again. My brain tries to take in everything, all of the senses flowing through my body, but it's too much.

I push him back, needing a breather, as I realize what he brought me up here to do. *Sex.* He brought me here to have sex.

Can I really go from having my first real kiss to having sex all in the same night?

Tristan's not a stranger. I've known him my entire life. He's got a bad-boy reputation of sleeping with girls and then leaving them. He wouldn't do that to me though. I mean more to him than that.

I look at his lust-filled eyes locked on my breasts, and I

know my answer. Yes, I will sleep with him. He won't hurt me. And I want him just as much as he wants me.

I seductively remove my shirt. I don't take my eyes off him as he takes a step back so he can take me in. His eyes grow with lust at seeing my bare skin. I watch him take his jacket off, followed by his shirt, exposing his muscles and tattoos I didn't know he had.

I walk closer to him and begin shimmying out of my skirt until I'm standing in just my underwear in front of Tristan, who is still wearing his jeans. I walk until I'm just in front of him and grab ahold of his jeans. He curiously looks down at me but doesn't say anything.

I slowly undo the button on his jeans, followed by the zipper. And then I slide his jeans down until they are around his ankles. To my surprise, he isn't wearing any underwear, and I can't keep the gasp from escaping my lips at the sight of him, at my first sight of a naked man.

He grins at my response. He takes my hand and guides me to it until I'm firmly grasping his cock in my hand. I stroke it once and watch as he moans at my touch. His hand stays on mine as he guides my hand up and down showing me what to do and how he likes it.

I must begin to be doing it right, because after a few more strokes he removes his hand from mine and moans loudly as I continue stroking. His hand goes to the back of my head pushing it down to his cock.

"Open your mouth," he says.

I do, and he pushes his cock inside. It's a strange feeling having him inside my mouth, and now I'm even more clueless as to what to do than I was before. I don't have to do much though as he pumps his cock in and out of my mouth. I gag once, but when I hear how loudly he moans with each thrust, I don't care he is making me gag. I want him to enjoy this.

He thrusts again, and then he moans, "Kinsley," as salty cum fills my mouth.

I swallow, wipe my mouth, and stand to see him grinning wildly at me.

He tucks my hair behind my ear and firmly kisses me on the cheek. I smile at him, but I'm not done with him yet. I want more. I want everything.

I move to the bed and lie down. "Come here," I say, patting the bed with lust in my eyes, trying to show him I want more without saying it.

He smiles at me and begins walking to the side of the bed. The door to the bedroom flies open before he gets to me. I grab the throw blanket on the edge of the bed and use it to cover myself as best as I can. When I glance at the door, I see Eli standing in the doorway, wide-eyed.

Eli glances at a naked Tristan, and his face turns furious. "Get out," Eli says to Tristan.

Tristan walks over to his jeans and casually slips them on, like he's not in a rush at all. He grabs his T-shirt from the floor.

"Tristan..." I say from the bed.

He turns to face me with a smile on his face. "The moment has passed, Kinsley. I'll let you get dressed and meet you downstairs."

I nod at his reassuring words. I won't be sleeping with Tristan tonight—well, at least, not right now—but I do plan on sleeping with him.

I watch as Tristan walks past Eli. The men glare at each other, and then Eli shuts the door, leaving me alone in the bedroom with nothing but my disappointment to give me comfort.

I quickly get up and get dressed. I put the blanket back on the bed as it was so the room doesn't look like it was disturbed. Although, after a night like tonight, I'm sure the whole house will look disturbed.

I'm just about to leave when I spot Tristan's jacket lying on the floor. I pick it up and put it on. I take a deep breath of the sleeve, trying to get any scent of the man I'm in love with. A man I've been in love with since I was twelve—or maybe earlier, if I'm honest with myself.

I walk out the door to a waiting Eli. I frown at him as I walk past. He grabs my arm, trying to stop me.

"Why did you do that?" I snarl at him.

"He's not good enough for you."

I roll my eyes and keep walking. "You don't get to make that decision."

I know Eli is following me as I make my way downstairs, but I don't care. All I need to do is find Tristan again. Once I'm back in his arms, everything will be right again.

I grab another beer as I make my way through the house. I need more alcohol in my system after one of the best nights of my life was interrupted by a man I don't care about. I drink my beer as I search the main floor of the house for Tristan.

After walking the entire main floor, I haven't spotted him, but I have finished my beer. I place the empty cup on the counter in the kitchen and head back to the living room to get another beer. I search for Tristan the entire time, but I still don't find him.

"He's outside," Eli says from behind me.

I turn slowly and narrow my eyes, not understanding why he would help me find Tristan when he just inter-rupted us.

"Thank you," I say anyway.

I grab another beer and begin walking toward the back door that leads outside to find him. The walk turns into a run as I can't wait to find him, but it takes me longer than I want to get to him due to the number of people I have to push through.

I finally get to the back door, and I slowly walk out to the warm summer air. I walk past the dance floor where Tristan and I were dancing earlier, but I don't spot him.

High-pitched squeals get my attention though, even over the booming music. I turn to see what the squealing is about when I see Vanessa in the pool with several of her girlfriends. Tristan throws her before swimming after her. I watch as he surfaces again, grabs ahold of Vanessa, and kisses her on the lips.

I drop my beer at the sight of him kissing another girl so quickly after me.

Tristan's eyes meet mine for just a second, and for just a moment, I see an ounce of worry there. He lets go of Vanessa, and to my surprise, he begins swimming toward me, like there is anything he could say to make this better.

He *used* me. He got what he wanted from me, and now, he is moving on.

I turn to go back into the house just as the tears fall, but I won't let him see that. He doesn't get to know that he hurt me, but he knows he did. That's why I hear him calling my name. Even as I run back into the house, I can still hear my name being repeated over and over.

Only once I'm back in the living room does his voice disappear, and it becomes replaced by my sobs. I spot Eli walking toward me, but I'm not ready to face him. Not yet. Not when he was right, and I was wrong.

I should have chosen Eli instead of Tristan. Eli is light while Tristan is dark, and I chose the darkness, thinking I could find the light in him. I couldn't though. He betrayed me the first chance he got.

I keep walking, needing to get out of the house. I need to go home. I make it to the entryway when I begin to hear sirens in the distance, growing louder with each second.

Shortly after, someone yells, "Cops!"

All at once, the house turns to panic as underage high schoolers begin pushing their way to get out of the house before the police arrive. I'm pushed out of the house in the process, but I don't have time to call for a ride like I was planning. I can't run. Not in my heels. I wouldn't make it far enough to escape being picked up by the cops for underage drinking.

I feel around in Tristan's pocket, hoping his car keys are there. I feel the bag he picked up at my father's casino. I try the other pocket and smile slyly when I find the keys, giving me just enough relief from the tears staining my face.

I move as fast as I can toward his car parked on the street. I climb in and start the engine, not feeling at all guilty that I'm taking his car while he'll be stuck to deal with questions from the cops about his drinking. I don't care. He deserves much worse after what he just did to me.

I start the car and step on the gas. The wheels squeal as I turn the corner, making it off the street just as I see the lights of cop cars turning onto the street where the party is going on. I smile, wiping the tears that are almost gone from my eyes.

I won't cry over that jackass. I glance down and realize I'm still wearing the asshole's jacket. I immediately take it off while keeping an eye on the road and speeding toward my house. I throw the jacket onto the passenger side. That's when I see it—the damn little black bag he picked up in the casino.

Now that I no longer lust for Tristan to distract me, I feel my curiosity grow until I can't wait any longer to find out what is in the bag. I grab the bag and fumble with the opening, but the string doesn't budge.

"Ah, come on," I curse at the bag that doesn't open.

I try again, pulling harder on the string until the bag pops open. White powder falls from the bag and onto my lap.

"What the hell?"

I try to dust myself off, but it's no use. I'm covered in white powder.

My mind finally makes the connection.

It's cocaine.

That's what Tristan was doing at the casino—buying drugs.

He's not who I thought he was. Not at all.

Tristan's a horrible, vile man who is nothing more than a druggie.

I throw the bag of drugs into the front seat and watch more powder fall onto the seat. My dream since I was twelve is gone. Shattered into dust, just like the dust of the cocaine scattered around his car.

I drive faster as my anger overtakes me. I can't believe I was so stupid. I can't believe I made such a ridiculous mistake going after Tristan. *Stupid, stupid!* I hit my hand against the wheel.

I round a corner, passing the busy section of downtown, when everything begins moving in slow motion. A child takes a step off the curb onto the street in front of me. I slam on the brakes, but my movement is too slow, slower than it should be. I turn the wheel, but the wheel moves even slower than the brakes.

I hear a woman scream.

I see the car miss the boy by no more than an inch.

Then, the car crashes into a light pole.

I feel my body jerk forward but am stopped abruptly as the airbag hits me.

Then, suddenly, everything moves fast. Much too fast. Sirens sound and approach quickly. I climb out of the car without a scratch on me. But it's not me I'm concerned with anymore. I glance across the street to the woman tightly holding her child with tears streaming down her face.

I could have killed her child. I could have taken away everything precious to her. And all because I made one bad decision after the next. A cop car approaches cautiously and stops just a few feet from where I'm standing.

He climbs quickly out of the car and runs over to me. "Is everyone okay? What happened?" he asks with a calm yet commanding voice.

I glance at the car and then back to the policeman. The car is filled with drugs. I've been drinking while underage and probably had more than the legal limit. I drove a car no one gave me permission to drive. I almost killed a child.

I'm going to jail. That much, I'm sure of. And I don't know when I'll be getting out.

I glance at the child who is visibly shaking in his mother's arms.

"You need to check on that child. You need to make sure he is okay," I say, gathering my courage, as I stare at the precious boy who, by some miracle, was spared. It had nothing to do with my ability to control a vehicle and everything to do with a miraculous event. "And then you need to arrest me."

3
____

KILLIAN

KINSLEY'S FACE when Agent Phillips called me Agent Byrne will forever be ingrained in my memory. Her gasp will forever be burned into my ears. The way her mouth fell open at his words before quickly turning into a grimace will haunt my dreams. Her beautiful bright eyes full of hope moments before turned to dark orbs that immediately shut me out of her life and her heart. It was a look I never wanted to see on her face.

I watched as Kinsley was placed in the back of one of our SUVs and driven away. The pain I felt at seeing her headed toward a jail cell hurt worse than I could've imagined. I never wanted this.

I turn to Agent Hayes, who is walking toward the second SUV. "This wasn't supposed to happen. Kinsley wasn't supposed to be arrested."

Agent Hayes stops and looks at me. "We have evidence she was colluding with her father and grandfather."

"What? You know that's not true. You know there is no way in hell that woman had anything to do with her family's criminal behaviors. They won't even let her run any part of the company. They won't let her decide what food to put into her mouth without questioning her first. She isn't involved in this."

Agent Hayes shakes his head. "You've gotten too close to the girl. Too close to make a reasonable judgment about her."

I run my hand through my hair in frustration. "My feelings for her have nothing to do with this. She's innocent."

He frowns at me and climbs into the driver's seat. I climb into the passenger seat next to him, and he quickly begins driving.

"She might be naive, but that doesn't make her innocent," he says.

"Why did you guys move in tonight? You were supposed to give me more time to gain his trust, so I could find out if they were hiding anything more."

"You're delusional. You've been undercover for too long. There was nothing left to find. The decision was made to move in before Lee Felton died, just like his son. Otherwise, we would have had no one left to prosecute, other than the granddaughter."

"You shouldn't be prosecuting her."

"That's not for you to decide."

I take a deep breath, trying to remain calm. No one will listen to me if I flip out, even though I'm the one who's been undercover for five years. I'm the one who should be making the decisions, not them, but I've made one too many mistakes in my past to be trusted.

"Offer her a plea deal then," I say.

"What?" Hayes glances from the road to me as we stop at a red light.

"Offer her a deal. Kinsley walks if she testifies against her grandfather."

He scrunches his nose. "But we don't need her to testify against her grandfather. We have enough evidence to convict him."

"Maybe, but he will have the best legal team money can buy. We need to be sure."

He looks back to the road and drives again as the light turns green. "I will see what I can do."

I take another deep breath, trying to relax, but it's impossible when I know Kinsley is on her way to a jail cell. A cell she will be stuck in for at least tonight, possibly much longer. A deal would at least give her a chance at freedom.

"You must be excited about getting a break now that your undercover stint is over. As soon as the trials are over, you will be able to go home for a while or go on a vacation."

I nod, but I'm not excited. I don't know where my home is anymore. I don't want to leave Las Vegas, not now that I've met the girl who has haunted my dreams for five years. I thought she was a naive, scared little girl. I thought she was weak and not able to make a decision for herself. I was wrong.

I've been a part of countless arrests. Every single person I've arrested or seen arrested had fear in their eyes when it happened. Every. Single. One.

Not Kinsley though. She faced being arrested head-on without a drop of fear on her face.

She stood up to her grandfather, a man I know to be a criminal.

She survived her father's death without losing any more of herself.

I was wrong about Kinsley. She's not just a princess. She's also a survivor. And possibly even a warrior.

But as much as I'm afraid I've fallen for her, I can't be her future. I can't be with her and still be with the FBI. As soon as she finds out the truth, she will hate me anyway. My future is with the FBI while her future...well, her future is with anything but me.

4

———

KINSLEY

THE DOOR to the holding cell opens, jarring me awake. I look around and find a third woman sitting in the holding cell with us. I rub my neck that is sore from sleeping against the hard, cold wall all night.

"Kinsley Felton," the officer says.

I stand and feel my knees crack from sitting all night.

"Come with me, please," he says.

The man leads me out of the room and into another room just down the hall. A room for questioning. The same room I was in last time.

He indicates for me to take a seat in the metal chair at the table. I sit down and wait for the door to open again. I pick at the rust on the metal table, just like I did last time, while I wait in the dark gray-colored room. I don't have to wait long.

My lawyer walks through the door, followed by FBI agents.

Our family lawyer, Mr. Greene, takes a seat next to me. "Don't worry, Ms. Felton. They have nothing to hold you on. I'll be able to get you out of here today."

I nod, and then my eyes widen at the men sitting across from me. Both men are from the poker game—Grant and Stephen. Grant still looks as cocky as ever, sitting across from me. The only difference is, his blond hair has recently been buzzed short. Stephen looks exactly the same—tall with buzzed short black hair.

"We meet again, Ms. Felton," Grant says.

I frown at him. "Except we weren't properly introduced last time we met." I turn to Stephen. "I'm guessing you aren't Killian's brother-in-law." I turn to Grant. "And I'm guessing you aren't a world champ at poker."

He smiles at me. "I guess not. I'm Agent Hayes, and this is Agent Liddell."

I don't smile at them. I glance at the door behind them, waiting to see if Killian will be walking through the door.

"He won't be coming," Agent Hayes says, reading my thoughts.

I frown at him but don't say anything further.

"So, here is the deal, Kinsley. We have physical evidence that could put you in jail for ten to fifteen years on fraud and money laundering charges. Your signature is all over all sorts of documents, proving you were involved in your grandfather's and father's legal troubles," Agent Hayes says.

I narrow my eyes. "What do you mean? My father and grandfather weren't doing anything illegal."

My lawyer places his hand on my arm, reminding me to let him do the talking. But I can't, not when my family is at stake.

"We've arrested your grandfather. He would be sitting in a jail cell right now if it wasn't for his need for medical attention. And your father would have been in a cell as well," Agent Hayes says.

I gasp at his words.

He continues speaking, "We have been investigating your whole family for the past five years. Your family has come into lots of money, more money than possible based on the income of your company.

"We've had undercover agents planted in the company. Agent Byrne was able to infiltrate your family to the fullest extent. We have evidence to convict your grandfather on many high-felony charges, including money laundering and fraud. He's looking at twenty-five-plus years," Agent Hayes says.

That can't be true. My family would never do anything illegal. We have always earned our money justly. Granddad is a stern man, and he would never do something like this. And I know my father wouldn't have.

The FBI is wrong, all wrong.

"But I wouldn't worry about your grandfather right now. I would worry about your own future. Ten-plus years. Based on your past transgressions, we might even get you on more," Agent Hayes says.

I glare at the man sitting across from me.

"You can't bring that up. It was buried five years ago."

Agent Hayes smiles. "Everything can be brought back up. Now, we can make this all go away for you. We can make it so you walk free today and never have to come back here."

"How?"

"All you have to do is agree to testify against your grand-father," Agent Hayes says.

"No," I say automatically. "I won't hurt my family."

He turns to my attorney.

"No. You don't have anything to charge Ms. Felton with, except some forged signatures that can be easily proven not to be hers. She is not taking a plea deal," Mr. Greene says.

"Then, we will bring the charges against her and go to trial," Agent Hayes says.

Mr. Greene leans over and whispers in my ear, "Do you know of anything that could incriminate your grandfather?"

"No," I whisper back.

He nods and turns back to the men. "What would you want my client to testify about?"

"We have reason to believe she knew of the actions of her father and grandfather, and while she didn't necessarily partake in the criminal activity, she knew exactly what was happening. We need her to testify to meetings she attended that occurred between her father and grandfather," Agent Liddell says.

"No," I say again.

"Think about it," Agent Liddell says, looking at my lawyer instead of me.

My lawyer whispers in my ear again, "Right now, I know I can get you out on bail. I wouldn't take the plea. But it is something to consider if the evidence is as strongly against you as they claim."

I nod but don't accept that. I don't accept that I might need to take a plea when, this time, I did nothing wrong. And I'd rather go to jail and think of it as penance for my past transgressions than say anything against my family.

"Is that all?" I ask.

"In a hurry to get back to your cell?" Agent Hayes asks.

"It's better than being in here."

"Your arraignment is scheduled to start in an hour. In the meantime, think about taking the plea. I'd hate to see a pretty woman like you end up spending the best years of your life in prison," Agent Hayes says.

Everyone stands, and an officer leads me back to the

holding cell but not before I get one last glare in at the agents.

I walk down the hallway leading back to the holding cell, the entire time scanning the area for Killian. He's the reason I'm here. Whatever he found, that's why I'm here, and it's why my grandfather is handcuffed to his bed.

And, as soon as I get out of here, I plan on finding Killian. I plan on finding out the truth.

5

KINSLEY

"HERE ARE the conditions of your bond. Read it carefully, and then sign here," the officer says, pointing to the bottom of the paper.

I take the pen and sign my signature without reading it. The same signature is supposedly all over several criminal papers. It's the reason I was locked up for almost twenty-four hours in the first place. It's the reason I could go to jail for ten years.

I slide the paper back to the officer, trying not to think about it when there are so many things I don't know or understand. Things I don't believe to be true. I don't believe my grandfather or my father would have done anything illegal, especially when it came to the well-being of their company.

"Here are your belongings." The officer slides over my phone, ID, and lip gloss—the only things I had on me when I was arrested.

I take them and put them in the pocket of my sweatpants. I tuck my long blonde hair behind my ear. It feels tangled and greasy from not showering.

"You're free to leave then."

I turn from the officer and walk out the door of the jail. I take a deep breath to keep the tears at bay as I walk out into the warm Las Vegas air.

"Oh my God! Are you okay?" Scarlett says, running toward me.

She immediately wraps her arms around me, like I've been off at war for a few years instead of just sitting in a holding cell for one night.

"I'm fine, Scar."

She releases me and begins looking me up and down. She inspects every inch of me, but I don't know what she expects to find. I'm not bleeding or permanently scarred. I didn't get any tattoos or join a gang.

"I'm fine," I repeat.

She suspiciously eyes me, like she doesn't believe me. "You should get a doctor appointment just in case."

I roll my eyes at her and start walking toward the car she drove to pick me up. "I'm fine."

"You don't know that for sure. You could have caught hepatitis or something while you were in there."

"Scar," I whine, "I'm fine."

I give her a stern look before I quickly walk the rest of the way to the car. Scarlett scurries behind me in her heels. Each step of her heels makes a loud clicking on the concrete making me jumpy. You never know when a strange man is coming to put me in handcuffs again.

I open the door to her red Mercedes two-door coup, feeling exhausted and tired. I just need to go home and sleep. Everything will make sense after a good night's sleep. Even though it's two or maybe three in the afternoon, it feels like two or three in the morning to me; that's how exhausted I am. I just need to sleep for twenty hours straight, and then I'll wake up and realize this was all a dream.

I move to slide into the passenger seat, but something makes me stop. I don't know why I look behind me, but I do. I think I'll always look behind me, keeping one eye open when I sleep because anyone could betray me at any time.

When I look up, I realize why I had the feeling as I see Killian standing just outside the jail building. He intensely looks at me, like he always does. His dark brown hair looks a little unkempt on top of his head, and it's obvious he hasn't shaved since the last time I saw him. He's dressed in a suit, much the same as he has been almost every day I've spent with him. Every day, except for the one day he took me on a date, but it wasn't really a date. It was just a way for the other agents to try to get information from me. It was just a hoax.

I feel my anger bubbling inside me, I slam the door, and my feet begin moving toward him before I even have a chance to think about what I'm doing.

"Kins?" Scarlett asks hesitantly.

"I'll be right back," I say as I continue to walk toward Killian.

He keeps his overpowering eyes on me, his face not showing me any emotion or giving anything away as I walk to him. When I get close, he indicates for me to follow and then begins walking away from the building. We walk two blocks before he ducks into an alleyway and stops, turning to face me.

"You okay?" he asks.

I roll my eyes. "I'm fine." I'm annoyed that everyone keeps asking me that. "Why are we here?"

"We couldn't have this conversation in front of the jail.

Too many cameras and witnesses." He pauses. "I'm not supposed to speak to you. It's not good for the case."

"I see. Then, why are you?" I raise my eyebrows.

He innocently looks at me. "Because I couldn't stay away."

I open my mouth to speak, but Killian's lips crash with mine, and I stumble backward in shock. He easily catches me in his arms, as if he was expecting my reaction. His lips are brutal against mine, demanding more from me. Even though our last kiss was just last night, it feels like we haven't kissed in years. The kiss feels like home, something I'm desperate for after spending a night in jail.

Those feelings quickly go away though as thoughts of last night creep back into my head. I try to lose myself in the kiss again and pretend there is nothing wrong. That he wasn't the reason I just spent a night in jail even though I had done nothing wrong. I want to love him, but instead, I hate him.

I try to push Killian back to get him to release my lips so I can show him I hate him, and I no longer care about him. He doesn't budge though. He kisses me harder, making it even harder to resist. Every kiss brings me closer to giving in to him and forgetting my hatred. So, instead, I decide to attack back with my own defiant and brutal kisses. I bite and nip and pull at his lips as my hands claw at his back.

He doesn't fight me. He lets me take my anger out on him, as if he thinks he deserves the pain I'm inflicting. He does. He deserves worse after lying to me and my family. He deserves a whole lot worse.

I bite down hard this time, hard enough to draw blood and for him to let go of me. He touches his fingers to his lips and then removes his hand, looking at the blood. His eyes then look to me, and I see the lust still in his eyes. He still wants me, but he doesn't love me. He doesn't care about me. If he did, he would have told me what was going on before he had me arrested. He wouldn't have let me get so invested in him when he wasn't being truthful. He was using me.

"What was that?" I ask.

"It was a kiss. It was—"

"Stop. I don't want to hear it. We are over. It doesn't matter what it was."

Killian sucks in a breath but doesn't argue with me.

"Why have you been investigating my family?"

He blankly looks at me but doesn't say anything.

"What did you find?"

Again, he stands stoic and doesn't answer.

"Why did you propose to me? Why did you try to become CEO? Why was I in jail? Why? Just...why?"

He doesn't answer me or show any reaction to my questions.

"My family did nothing wrong. Not my grandfather. Not me. And especially not my father." I don't know why I feel the need to defend my father now that he's dead, but I do. I think I feel even stronger about fighting for him because I loved him more than anyone, and he's not here to defend himself. I won't let his memory become tarnished.

"How long have you been investigating? The full five years you have been working for the Felton Corporation?"

He doesn't answer me, but there is one question that he might answer—one question he owes me.

"What is your name? Your real name?"

I wait for Killian to answer, to say anything about what happened.

He doesn't. He just looks longingly at me.

I shake my head as I begin pacing back and forth in the

small alleyway. It must have rained last night because I notice a small puddle of water as I walk through it.

"You owe me your name, don't you think? We slept together. You proposed to me. Don't you think you owe me your name?"

His eyes soften and sadden at my words. I've affected him but not enough for him to talk to me or tell me anything.

"If you're not going to talk to me, then why am I here?"

Killian isn't going to tell me anything. I really wasn't anything to him. Just someone he could sleep with to make his time undercover more enjoyable.

He moves his hand to touch me, but I brush it away. He doesn't get to touch me again if he's not going to talk to me.

"I came to say good-bye. I won't come to speak to you again—at least, not outside of a courtroom or FBI building."

He hesitates, and I feel tears welling in my eyes at the thought that I might never see him again. Even now that I know the truth, it doesn't stop me from getting emotional at the thought I might never see him again outside of a courtroom or interrogation room. It won't be like this again.

"And I came to say I'm sorry. I never meant to hurt you or to let you get so emotionally invested. I was just trying to do my job. I never wanted this. You understand why we can't be together? Why we have to say good-bye now?"

I nod. "I understand that you never cared about me and were only doing your fucking job!" Anger escapes my mouth with my words. I was trying to hide it because as long as I was hiding it, he wouldn't know how much he truly hurt me.

He winces, feeling hurt by my words.

I close my eyes, trying to calm myself before I speak again. When I open my eyes, I say the only words I have left to say, and I say them without any emotion, despite the pain I feel inside, "Good-bye, Killian."

"Good-bye, princess." He opens his mouth to say more, but then he stops himself. He turns to walk away, but then he stops and walks back to me, like he's changed his mind again. "Take the deal they are offering you. You don't deserve to go to jail. I don't want to have to testify against you. If this goes to trial, you will go to jail. Take the deal."

"You're incredible. You don't tell me anything. You lie to me the entire time I've been with you, and then you tell me to give up everything I've ever known. You're just trying to get me to testify against my grandfather. I won't do it."

"You have to trust me on this. They will nail you. They have the evidence they need, and your grandfather will go to jail, no matter if you testify or not. So, take the deal. There is no reason to sacrifice yourself just to be loyal to a family who has never been loyal to you."

I shake my head. "No."

He grabs my shoulders. "Please, just listen to me."

"Why should I? You won't answer any of my questions. Not one single question. I don't even know who you are."

His eyes look sad. He removes his hands from my shoulders and runs one hand through his hair in frustration. "That's what I thought."

I look at him for one second longer. Just long enough to remember everything. His intense brown eyes. His lips that hardly ever smile. The rough stubble of his five o'clock shadow and every muscle flexing against his suit jacket.

And then I walk away without saying another word. I begin walking back down the street to find Scarlett when I feel his hand on my shoulder.

"Wait."

I turn and look at him. He pants, catching his breath.

"My name is Liam Killian Byrne, but everyone calls me Killian."

His eyes tell me he's being honest. He's not bluffing. I studied him long enough at the poker table to know when he was lying or telling the truth, but I don't thank him for offering me that one piece of honesty. Instead, I turn away from him and continue to walk to Scarlett's Mercedes. He might have told me his real name, but that's not enough for him to earn my forgiveness. I won't ever forgive him if my grandfather goes to jail and my father's company is lost in scandal.

"You okay?" Scarlett asks as I open the car door and slide in.

"I'm fine," I say for what seems like the millionth time.

Scarlett hesitantly steps on the gas.

I'm not fine though. I just said good-bye to a man my heart is still beating for. I said good-bye to a man I still love, despite everything.

I shake my head. I chose Tristan, and it was the worst mistake of my life. I chose Eli, but he couldn't stand up to my family's scrutiny. My father chose Killian, and now he's going to tear our family apart.

I don't know how to choose my future. And I don't trust my family to choose either. I don't even know what my choices are. All I know is, I have to keep my grandfather from spending the rest of his life in jail. And I have to keep the Felton Corporation from being torn apart by the FBI. I will have to spend the rest of my life alone. I can't face the possibility of choosing wrong again.

6

KILLIAN

I WALK BACK into the FBI building across the street from the jail we were holding Kinsley in. I'm surprised to be welcomed with hooting and hollering when I walk inside.

Several people shake my hand and congratulate me as I walk through the lobby. The building is full of people whom I hardly know and have barely worked with at all in the last five years, but they feel the need to congratulate me.

I continue walking through until I reach the door that says *Agent Bisson* on the door, my boss's office. I knock before entering and find him sitting behind his desk. When he sees me, he stands and walks over to me with a smile on his face.

"Excellent work," Agent Bisson says.

I nod and attempt to move my lips up into a smile, but instead, they stubbornly remain pursed.

"You've more than earned the promotion coming your way."

"What?"

"You'll be promoted to senior agent after this is all over. You've more than earned it."

"Thank you, sir."

I'm not sure what to think. I've worked for five years to get this promotion. My father will be more than proud. It's always what he wanted out of a son, but when my boss told me I was getting a promotion, I felt nothing.

That's not a normal response to a promotion. I should feel excited or happy or proud, not indifferent.

I hear him talking about what my promotion will entail, but I don't really hear him. I'm lost in my own world and thoughts again. Lost in Kinsley and what should have been.

I should have gotten more time with her. More time to earn her trust and make her fall for me. I've fallen for her. I fell for her almost three years ago when I broke up her relationship with Eli, but it wasn't until I met her, not until I had her, that I realized how hard I had fallen.

I thought I had time. Time to allow her to fall just as hard for me. So hard that, when I told her the truth, it wouldn't matter because she'd know I loved her. I thought we could make it work and she would never be arrested. Now, I'll never know.

"You've more than made up for your past indiscretions, Agent Byrne."

"Thank you, sir."

"You going home over your four weeks off after the trials are over?"

"Yes, sir."

"Good, I wish we could give you longer than four weeks. You deserve longer after five-plus years, but it's all I can give you right now. We have too many open cases and not enough undercover agents."

I nod somberly.

"Cheer up, son. You're a hero around here right now, and you'll be able to leave on break soon. If their lawyers are smart, they will negotiate a deal when they see the evidence you collected against them. With any luck, it won't go to trial, and you will get to take your break in a matter of weeks. If not, you should be able to go in a few months once your testimony is done."

I nod, unable to speak about the fact that I know Kinsley won't take the plea deal as much as I want her to. She won't betray her family. She won't leave and take the easy route as much as I want her to. And her grandfather is a stubborn man. He won't go to jail either without a fight.

"Is that all, sir?"

"Yes, and don't forget to set up a meeting with the prosecutor tomorrow to begin preparing for trial, just in case."

"I will, sir."

I walk back out of his office and head to the main floor, the whole time thinking of Kinsley instead of what I'm going to do next. All this time, I've been living in a hotel room at the Felton Grand. I'll have to find an apartment now because I can't see her again.

"Stop it," Agent Hayes says to me.

I glance up at him, not understanding.

"Stop thinking about her. You can't have her. It would ruin your career and the case. You have to stay away from her."

"I don't know what you are talking about."

"Sure you do. I saw you with her outside the jail. I read your reports that were biased toward her. Stay away from her, or you'll end up in a jail cell yourself."

I glare at him but don't argue. He's right. I can't have it both ways. I'm either loyal to the FBI or her.

"I have a report to write."

"Good, see that you write it without telling the whole FBI that you love her. Here's your ID and FBI badge."

I roll my eyes at him and take them from him. Choosing the FBI means I'll be returning to a life I haven't known in five years. While I was undercover, I got to pretend I was someone else and could put the past behind me. Now, I have to face my life head-on. A life I never wanted to return to, filled with more pain than I can bear. A life that is no longer who I am.

7

KINSLEY

SCARLETT PULLS into the driveway of the house I grew up in. I've been living in a hotel room at the Felton Grand, but I can't go back there. It would remind me too much of Killian, and I can't handle thinking about him.

I get out of the car without talking to Scarlett. I haven't spoken to her since I got in the Mercedes, despite her incessant trying. I just couldn't.

I throw the front door open without testing the lock first. It's almost always unlocked. I run up the stairs two at a time and run down the hallway to my childhood bedroom. I run to my bed and collapse on it just as the tears begin burning in my eyes.

I hear Scarlett come in, but I still don't say anything to her. I'm not sure what she is going to do, but then I feel her wrap her arms around me as she lies next to me on the bed. She doesn't say anything further, and she doesn't try to question what happened or why I'm crying.

I let everything out. I let the fear out I felt while I was sitting in the holding cell. I let the worry out at realizing my grandfather and father could have done something illegal. I let the pain out Killian caused me. I let it all go.

And, when it's all out almost an hour later, I finally speak, "I still love him."

"I know," Scarlett says.

"I can't go to jail."

"You won't. You did nothing wrong."

"Granddad can't go to jail either."

Scarlett doesn't respond. Instead, the room is eerily silent.

"Scar?" I say, sitting up.

She stares down at my comforter.

"Granddad can't go to jail. They can't ruin my father's memory."

Scarlett hesitantly looks up at me. "But what if he did something? What if he did lie and cheat and smuggle money or whatever they are charging him with? What if he deserves to go to jail? What if your father helped him?"

I stand from the bed. "He didn't do anything. Neither of them did!"

Scarlett gets up. "But what if they did? The FBI wouldn't have arrested your grandfather if he didn't do something wrong."

"They arrested *me*, and *I* didn't do anything wrong."

Scarlett doesn't say anything, but she looks guilty, like what she wants to say next is going to hurt. She opens her mouth to say the words anyway, "But you did do something wrong, Kins, or they wouldn't have arrested you. Even if you didn't mean to. Even if you were just doing whatever your father or grandfather had asked of you, you did something. You were just too naive to know what you were doing."

"Get out!"

Scarlett looks at me in shock.

I walk over to my bedroom door and open it, indicating for her to get out. I'm not going to listen to her blame my father or Granddad or me for what's happened.

"Get out," I say firmly.

She sighs and picks her purse up off the floor where she must have dropped it before climbing onto my bed.

"Call me when you realize I'm right."

I don't say anything, even though I think of several comebacks I would like to say to her. We've been friends too long, and I know, deep down, she is just saying what she believes to be true. I just can't believe her words.

I walk back to my bed, planning on sleeping the rest of the day away. I try to sleep—God knows I need it—but I end up tossing and turning.

Killian. I want to call him and see him, but I can't. Killian is gone, replaced by Liam. That's his name. Liam. Killian doesn't exist. Just like everything that happened between wasn't real.

I take out my phone while I wait for my pancakes. I type in his name—*Liam Killian Byrne*. Nothing comes up though. Not a Facebook page. Or Twitter. Not a mention of a school he attended—just nothing.

I sigh in frustration and put my phone back in my pocket. I close my eyes trying to fall asleep again. Maybe this nightmare would end if I slept.

After trying for three hours to fall asleep, I get out of bed and make my way downstairs. My mother is passed out on the couch with a fifth of tequila gripped in her hand.

I exhale. I can't deal with her right now. Tomorrow I'll take her to rehab. Tomorrow I'll find a solution to every-thing. Today I just need to find a way to keep breathing.

I continue walking on until I find myself in front of my grandfather's bedroom and push the door open.

The smell of his cigars immediately overwhelms me as I step inside. The furniture in the room is all dark oak. The comforter is shades of red. On each wall is all of my grandfather's accomplishments — a picture of every casino and hotel. I glance at his nightstand where there is a picture of his family. I must be no more than five in the picture. It was the last picture my grandmother was in. Lying next to it is a business book and his reading glasses.

I pick up the book. It's a book on leadership. I take the book onto the couch in the living room and open the book to the first page to begin reading.

Scarlett's wrong. Killian's wrong. The FBI's wrong. Granddad is a good man who loved the company. He would never have done anything to endanger it.

———

"What are you doing?" my mother asks when we are halfway to the rehab center.

"Getting you help."

"I'm not the one who needs help," she spits at me, referencing my current predicament with the law.

It is only a matter of time before she brings up the last time again.

At hearing my mother's words, I purse my lips but don't allow my anger to overtake me. I won't allow her to get to me like last time. But the memories of last time, the memories of five years ago, still ring in my ear.

The drive home from jail is long and silent. My father sits in the driver's seat, next to my grandfather. Neither of them has said a word to me since they picked me up, but from their expressions, I know they are disappointed in me, worse than disappointed in me. As soon as I walk through the door to our house, I will be lectured. I try to prepare myself for it as I sit in the back seat of the car, but I know I will deserve it or worse, and there is no way to prepare for it.

We pull up to our house. My father parks his Audi in the driveway, but none of us move to get out. None of us want to deal with what we all know must happen once we get inside.

We have to deal with the reality that I might go to prison. That the Felton Corporation is now under investigation for selling drugs since the man who gave Tristan the drugs was an employee. Since I was found with the drugs, that makes two people linked to the Felton Corporation.

The family of the boy I almost hit is suing. Once they found out how much money our family had, they decided to sue for emotional damages I caused the boy and mother.

Tristan's family is pressing charges against me for stealing and damaging his car.

There has been a wave of cancellations of events and bookings in our casinos and hotels after our family was portrayed as druggies and our hotels as drug rings. We are at risk of losing everything my family has worked for because of me.

Granddad is the one who finally decides it's time. He opens the door and climbs out. So, my father and I do the same. Still, no one says a word as we walk into the house.

That silence ends though as soon as my mother sees me.

"You fucking little shit," my mother says, striking me hard on the cheek while holding a bottle in her other hand.

It burns where she hit me, but the embarrassment and pain of being slapped by my mother at sixteen hurt worse than the physical pain. My father moves to stop my mother from doing it again, but out of the corner of my eye, I watch Granddad stop him. My mother slaps me again, but this time, I expected it, which somehow lessens the pain.

My mother raises her hand a third time.

"Enough," Granddad says.

My mother stops mid-air, and instead, she lifts the bottle of amber liquor to her lips, swallowing large gulps. "You stupid fucking child! You've fucking ruined everything!"

My mother storms over to my father, and as she walks by me, I smell the alcohol seeping out of her pores. She's had more than she should have, more than anyone should have.

"This is your fault," she says. Her face is red. "We should never have had her. I told you! I told you she would destroy the family!"

At my mother's cruel words, I feel tears falling, but she's right.

"Kinsley hasn't destroyed the family. She has merely provided a setback, but we will get through this, just like every other crisis our family has faced," my father says.

"Don't bullshit her! She has destroyed the family. We will recover—we always do—but Kinsley has effectively destroyed the image of the family and company. And, no matter what we do, the shame of public opinion will never go away. The question now is, what do we do with her? I say, throw her out on the streets. Disown her. Let her go to prison to pay for her crimes," my mother says.

"No, that won't do. It would make the family look worse. Boarding school perhaps?" Granddad says.

"Rehab?" my father suggests.

I feel more tears burn as my father suggests rehab. I never told him the drugs weren't mine. I never turned in Tristan. I just...couldn't. Not when I was so stupid to do what I did. Not when I almost killed someone for my stupid mistake.

"I'll do whatever you say. Whatever you want," I say.

The room falls silent.

"What do you mean?" Granddad asks.

"I made a mistake, a horrible mistake I will never forgive

myself for. I make horrible decisions. I chose a horrible person to date... I won't do it again."

Granddad smiles at me. "Excellent. Then, it's settled. You will speak to me or your father from now on before making any decisions, no matter how trivial. Do you understand?"

"Yes."

"And when the time comes, your father and I will choose the man you marry."

I nod.

"Good. Now, go to your room, and don't come out until dinner."

I nod and head off to my room, feeling better, knowing I will never make this horrible of a mistake again. I will never hurt my family or anyone else ever again. I will never choose whom I will date or fall in love with again.

My mother didn't drink again after that day. Father and Granddad got her help and convinced her, if she continued to drink, it would just further ruin the reputation of the family. She didn't drink again until my father's death.

Now, I have to put a stop to it. Not because she will destroy the family. Her drinking is the least of the family's worries at the moment, but because, deep down, I still love her. I don't want her to drink away her life any further.

I remember my promise. That I would never date or choose who I fell in love with again. I'd let my family do that. My family chose Killian though, and he turned out wrong, but I chose him, too. We both chose wrong. They all end up like this—with a broken heart and family.

I park the car in front of the rehab center, the same one she went to last time.

"Go inside," I say calmly to my mother.

She laughs. "I'm not going inside. I'm not the one in

trouble. I'm not the one who has done something stupid again and given up my freedom."

"No, you're right. I'm the bad apple in the family. But I'm not the only bad apple. It seems I come from a family of bad apples."

My mother moves to grab me, but I'm already prepared. I grab her arms, and in her drunken stupor, she is too weak to hurt me.

"Go inside, mother. Get clean. You won't get any money if we are all in jail unless you get clean."

That makes her pause for just a second. I shake my head. She didn't love my father like she told me. She loved his money.

"Go," I say again.

This time, she gets out of the car. I get out, too, as much as I don't want to, and I help her walk inside. I help her check herself in. And then I leave her to be taken care of by the rehab center. If only fixing the rest of my family's problems were so simple.

8

___

KILLIAN

I UNPACK the last of my boxes in my new apartment. I started at six a.m. and didn't have many boxes since I'd been living out of a hotel room for five years, so it's just thirty minutes later when I finish. The apartment is small compared to the luxurious hotel room I was staying in, but it will do for now.

I won't have the apartment for long anyway. Once the trials are over, I'll be on break for a few weeks where I can go home or go on vacation. And then I'll get a new assignment, which could be anywhere in the country.

So, this apartment will do. It's modern and fully furnished, and it does month-to-month leases. That's all that matters.

I grab a bottle of water from the fridge and chug it. I have time to work out before my meeting with the prosecutor this morning. I think about heading to the exercise room at the main building in the apartment complex, but I don't think working out indoors will be enough to distract me.

So, instead, I grab my headphones and connect them to

my phone. I turn on Spotify and pick the first playlist, which is Today's Hits. Then, I crank the music as loud as I can. I don't bother warming up. I run at full speed as soon as I make it out of my apartment building. I don't know the area well enough to know where I should run, so I just run through a neighborhood while focusing on my breathing and the music.

I breathe in and out to the beats of Adele, followed by The Weeknd and then Beyoncé. My speed matches the song that is playing, which means I run faster or slower, depending on the beat and not how my body feels. I listen to the lyrics, really concentrating on each word to keep every other thought out of my mind.

It works until Justin Bieber comes on, singing about how sorry he is to some girl, and I lose the rhythm of my breathing and running. I quickly lose my breath until I can't breathe or run. All I can do is listen to the lyrics of the song and think about how much Kinsley loves Justin Bieber. I might not be a fan of his music, but I will never be able to hear his songs again without thinking about her.

I walk back to my apartment, replaying the song over and over again in my head and picturing how I could say sorry to her. *How can I make it up to her?*

I can't though, and even if I could, I could never say sorry enough to make it up to her. Because *sorry* isn't enough after you've destroyed someone's family.

When I make it back to my apartment, I shower and change into a suit. The same suit I would wear when I went to work at the Felton Corporation. It feels weird to put it on and not go into work there. Instead, I'll be going to the FBI office.

I grab my laptop I used last night to finish my last report on the Felton case. I made sure it contained no feelings of empathy for the Felton family. I place the laptop in my briefcase and then head out to my Chevy Malibu rental car.

The drive to the FBI office building seems long. I'm used to just walking downstairs to my office at the Felton Corporation. I find a parking spot on the street and then make my way through the dry heat and into the building. People smile at me, but I don't return the pleasantries as I make my way through the building to the law offices where the prosecutor wants to meet. I don't understand the point in fake smiling when you don't feel like smiling. Although, with that attitude, I might never smile again because I'm not sure I'll ever be happy again.

I make it to the door of the prosecutor's office. The door is closed, but I don't bother knocking. It's one thing the FBI has taught me—to own my power as an agent. And walking into someone's office is a great way to show people I have power while also catching them off guard. I can see people in their real state instead of the fake demeanor they most often offer me.

The man behind the desk isn't fazed though as I walk into his office, unannounced. Working in an FBI building like this, full of agents who probably walk in on him all the time, probably did that to him.

He looks up at me but doesn't smile. I like this man already.

"Agent Byrne, I presume?"

"Yes." I extend my hand to him.

He takes it, and we shake.

"I'm Roy Fowler, the head prosecutor. Have a seat." Roy motions for me to take a seat opposite him.

"I've spent the last few months reading through all of your reports. Excellent job. This will be an easy open-and-shut case if you ask me. Honestly, I shouldn't even offer Ms.

Felton a deal because it's such an airtight case, but we did offer her a deal already. I could rescind it..."

"No!"

He looks at me with a confused expression, and I shut my mouth, realizing I can't stand up for her anymore, not here.

"I was saying I could rescind the deal, but I'm not going to. I don't think she was the ringleader in this. I think she was just doing what her family told her to, and she didn't even realize she was breaking the law.

"I've thought long and hard about Mr. Felton, and based on his age, I'm planning on offering him a deal for ten years. He'll easily get out in five to seven. The most important thing is for him to step down from running the company to ensure the company is now run legally."

I take a deep breath, realizing he isn't going to send Kinsley to jail. The offer he is going to make to her grandfather is more than fair. "I think that's fair."

He nods. "If they are smart, they will take the pleas, and this will be over this week, but if they decide to go to trial, I want you to be ready to testify. We could go to trial against Ms. Felton as soon as next week if she doesn't take the deal by tomorrow. Her acceptance of the deal or conviction, if it comes to that, will put the pressure we need on Mr. Felton. Either way, I don't think he will go to trial if she agrees to testify against him or ends up in jail herself."

I suck in a breath. It takes everything inside of me not to defend Kinsley.

"Anyway, here is a list of questions I will be asking you when you testify as well as some questions the defense might ask you about Ms. Felton. I want you to spend the morning going through them on your own. Then, this afternoon, I will have time to better prep you on your answers to ensure they are clear and concise."

I look down at the long list of detailed questions about Kinsley I don't want to answer, especially in front of a jury. "I understand."

I take the papers and leave the room, hating the fact that the rest of the day is going to be spent thinking about how I'd answer questions that could put Kinsley behind bars for at least ten years. I hope she's smart enough not to let it come to that.

I shake my head. It's not that she isn't smart enough. It's that she cares about her family too much. I have to find some way to convince her to take the deal before I am forced to send her to jail.

9

___

KINSLEY

Ten years.

That is the minimum prison sentence I face.

Ten years. Or longer.

I would be in my thirties when I got out of jail. All of my twenties would be wasted. I would have no chance of finding a career. No chance at finding out who I am while I'm young. No chance of falling in love before I'm thirty.

My lawyer said I could take a plea deal if I wanted. Testify against my grandfather, and I would be free.

I said no.

My lawyer agreed that not taking the plea deal was the best. But my lawyer also represents my grandfather. He's not looking out for what's best for me. He's looking out for what's best for Granddad.

But I won't take the plea deal to save myself. I have nothing to testify against Granddad anyway. And I don't think Granddad did anything wrong.

I may not trust my lawyer, but I do believe he can keep me out of jail. He's the best. We are paying him a ridiculous amount of money to defend us against something we shouldn't even be fighting. He will keep us out of jail.

A signature is the only evidence the FBI has against me anyway. My signature. One stroke of a pen.

My lawyer says it can easily be proven my signature was forged. That the entire documents are fake. I believe him. But it doesn't keep my stomach from tightening in knots as I drive away from my lawyer's office.

I catch movement out of the corner of my eye that draws my eye away from the road to the building next to me. A man in a sharp suit with an intense scowl on his face exits the building.

Killian.

He glances up, and our eyes meet. The pain from our last meeting comes flooding back. Pain. Anger. Hurt. Need. They all mix together until I have no idea which feeling is strongest.

Just the sight of him has my body twisted and aching. I didn't want to see him again, especially not so soon when I haven't persuaded my heart to let him go yet. But here he is, and I feel my heart begging me to pull the car over and run into his arms. Need grows in my belly, the need to kiss his lips again and take him back to my house so I can ride him until he satisfies my lust. I also feel the need to turn my car and run him over for what he has done to my family. I just don't know which of the three feelings is strongest—love, lust, or anger.

I don't get to decide which feeling is strongest. Fate and Killian decide for me. Killian breaks eye contact as he turns away from me. I glance back to the street, and the light is now green. So, I drive away from Killian. I say a second good-bye, keeping the tears buried deep inside. I don't know if I can bear to say good-bye again.

I have to find out the truth, and the only man I can find out the truth from is my grandfather. I have a million more questions that need to be answered. The only person who will be able to answer them is my grandfather. So that's where I'll go—to get the answers to the only questions that matter.

————

Granddad's hospital room looks the same as the last time I was here. There is just one marked difference. One of his arms is handcuffed to the bedrail. He can't even get out of bed on his own, but the officer decided to handcuff him anyway.

I run over to his side.

"Granddad," I say hesitantly as he lies in bed, seemingly asleep. I should let him rest if he is sleeping, but this can't wait. I need to know. I need to know as much as I can.

His eyes slowly open, and then he smiles when he sees it's me and not a nurse or doctor or police officer.

"Kinsley, I'm so glad you came. I heard they released you last night, but I wasn't sure if you would want to see me."

I take his frail hand in mine. "Of course I want to see you. You're my grandfather. I love you. You're the only family I have left."

He raises an eyebrow.

"I don't count Mother. I dropped her off in rehab this morning anyway. She needs to get better."

He pats my hand. "I'm glad you did that. She needs help."

"What about you? How are you doing?"

Granddad shrugs. "I've been better."

"They told me you are getting out of here tomorrow morning."

He nods but doesn't say anything more. He's not going to talk to me. He's not going to tell me what the hell we were both arrested for without me asking.

"What is going on? What happened? Why were we both arrested?"

He looks out the window of his hospital room without answering me. I give him a second to gather his thoughts, but I soon realize that is not what he is doing. He's avoiding me, not answering me, which surprises me. I thought, once I asked, he would answer, just like always, but I guess being faced with spending the rest of your life in jail changes a man.

"Granddad, did you and Dad do what they say you did? Did you lie and cheat to grow the company? Did you commit fraud and money laundering to build the company?"

Granddad's head whips to look at me. His face is red, and his nostrils are flared. "Hell no, we didn't do any of those things! I can't believe you would even ask me such a thing. You think your own grandfather would commit a crime? Your own father?"

"No," I say firmly. "I don't *want* to believe what the FBI says is true. I *don't* believe what they say is true. I just need to hear you tell me the truth. I need to know why I'm facing charges of crimes I didn't commit, why you are facing charges if you didn't commit the crimes either."

He takes a deep breath, and his face softens, the shade of red turning to pale pink. I hand him a cup of water from the bedside table, and he slowly sips it. His face returns to a normal shade instead of the burning fire that swept across his face moments ago.

"Why?" I ask again when he seems calmer. "Even our lawyer suspects you and Dad did this. What proof does the FBI have?"

"Five years ago, when you were arrested, and they found the drugs had come from one of our casinos, the FBI began investigating the company. They thought the company might be tied to a drug ring or something. It wasn't, but it made them very suspicious, suspicious enough to plant undercover agents in the company, except we didn't know that. We thought, when the FBI stopped talking to us about a year after your incident was over, they had found us innocent.

"Killian, the FBI agent they planted, never found anything. After five years, he never found anything, but the FBI couldn't give up after spending five years investigating us. Killian framed us because his superiors told him to. Killian had to prove himself to the FBI after he made a mistake that should have put him in jail."

"What mistake?"

"It doesn't matter. What matters is, you stay away from him. He's the enemy, not me. He's the criminal."

I nod. I believe the man sitting in front of me over the man who has lied to me.

"Good."

I watch my grandfather's movements the whole time he is talking, trying to decide if he is telling the truth or not. I don't know if he is telling the truth, but I feel like he is. I feel like he has to be, not because I believe my grandfather to be a good man, but because I know my father was a good man. My father wouldn't have committed a crime, and there is no way my grandfather could have done something like this without my father knowing.

"Don't worry about the company, Granddad. I just want you to focus on getting better and staying out of jail."

Granddad frowns, and I know he is going to protest.

"I still don't think you are strong enough or capable of running the company—"

I narrow my eyes at him. "You don't exactly have a choice. Killian was a terrible choice. You chose to give half of the company to the one man who had been working against you. Tony is a worse choice. There is no one else in a high enough position who can run it. At this point, it's me or nobody. I can do this. The mistakes I made were nothing compared to the mistakes others in this family have made."

Granddad winces as he reaches over to the bedside table and grabs a piece of paper. "I was going to say that, despite my reservations, you're right. I don't have a choice."

He hands me the piece of paper he had typed up, and I quickly read it. He is giving me temporary power over the company until he is healed and his trial is over.

"Thank you. I'll do you proud."

He smiles. "You will because you'll do everything I say."

I shake my head. "No, I won't. I'll do what is best for the company, no matter what that is. I'm not sure I have the best judgment in the world, but now, I know that it can't be any worse than yours. If I sign this, I want full authority over my life and the company. I want your trust. I don't want to be your puppet."

He thinks for a second and then smiles. "I was hoping you would say that."

He hands me a pen, and I hesitate over the papers.

Can one signature change your life? One signature, whether mine or not, sent me to jail. I'm about to find out for the second time if one signature changes everything.

10

KINSLEY

I PULL the car into the driveway of my family home. A home I feel both closer to and further away from. Closer because I feel like I have to rely more on my family in order to get through these next few months. And further away because I'm afraid the walls of this household secrets I'm not ready to face.

I turn off the car and walk over to the passenger door. I open it for Granddad and help him out of the car.

"Thanks, princess," he says.

I smile at him, not correcting him, just allowing him to use the name that only my father ever really called me.

And Killian...

Now, neither of those men will ever call me that again because both are out of my life.

"Just take it slow. No need to rush inside."

"I know I'm safe as long as you are by my side," he says.

I smile and nod at him as we walk slowly inside. I hope that is true. I hope I can stand by his side through everything coming our way.

I help him inside and to his bedroom and into bed. I

glance at the clock. I need to get to the casino. I scheduled some meetings for this afternoon to ensure everything has been running smoothly since his heart attack.

"I need to get going, but the nurse should be here soon, and I'll notify the staff to look in on you. Do you need anything before I go?"

"Where are you going?"

"To check on how things are going at the casinos."

He carefully eyes me. "Don't change anything without consulting me first."

I just smile. I don't argue with him. What he doesn't know won't hurt him.

"I have to go," I say before softly kissing him on the cheek.

I quickly run upstairs to change into something more appropriate for business. I slip on a business suit and heels, and then I run out the door to my car.

I am at the casino in a half hour.

When I walk up to the casino, I'm surprised by the crowd gathered outside. I watch as people pull out their phones when they see me walking into the casino. I try to smile brightly as they take my picture, seeming unfazed by the scandal swarming around my family.

I wave to the crowd at the door and then walk inside. I'm surprised to see the inside is just as crowded as the outside. I guess I expected no one would want to gamble or stay at a casino filled with scandal. Instead, it seems we have tripled our crowds overnight. I guess what they say is true; any press is good press.

I head straight to my father's office and close the door behind me. I walk over to the desk that is now covered in notes and papers people have dropped off, but no one has received because no one has been here. My father is gone. And now my grandfather. And Killian. That leaves me.

I quickly sort through the papers into things that need to be dealt with urgently and things that are less important.

Then, I dial Tony's number.

"Hello?" Tony says in confusion.

"Tony, it's Kinsley. Can you get everyone gathered in the meeting room in twenty minutes? I need to make sure everything is being handled since my grandfather and I were arrested."

"Sure, Ms. Kinsley."

"Thanks, Tony." I hang up the phone.

The last time I'd tried to run a meeting, it went horribly, horribly wrong. I don't even know what to say now, other than to make sure everyone is doing their job, especially since everyone who was anywhere near the CEO position is gone.

I gather every drop of strength I have as I stand, and I begin walking to the meeting room.

I have to walk past Killian's office on the way. I pause at the door that still says *Killian Browne* on the outside. The door is shut though, so I can't see inside. I don't know what I expect to see. He's not in there. And he never wanted me. He was just doing whatever the FBI had told him. He was getting my father and Granddad to trust him so he could find out whatever he thought they were hiding. That's it. Nothing more.

I have to think of Killian as nothing but a man who worked for the FBI. Just a man my family tried to get me to marry. Nothing between us was real, but it doesn't stop me from hoping he is somehow still in the office, just like he was the day I walked in with Tony.

I force myself to walk past his office to the meeting room

where Tony is waiting for me at the door. He smiles at me but doesn't say anything about the charges or situation I'm in. He just looks at me with a confident smile I match on my face.

"You ready?" he asks.

I take a deep breath, trying to channel every part of my father's strength inside me. "Yes."

Tony opens the door for me, and I confidently walk inside because I know I'm capable. I'm my father's daughter. I can do this.

Then, I glance around the room at the ten executives seated at the table, and I feel my anxiety creeping back in. I take a seat at the end of the long table.

But then Tony walks in with the same smile on his face, and I relax.

I can do this, I repeat over and over in my head.

"I called this meeting to…" I lose my train of thought as I feel everyone staring at me.

"You can do this," I feel my father telling me.

I take a deep breath and start again. This time, I look up at the men and women gathered around the table, and I feel calmer than I ever have.

"I called this meeting to discuss how things have been going since my grandfather had a heart attack and the sudden news that followed. I would like to hear from all of you about how things have been going and what ideas you have to keep the company moving forward during this diffi-cult time for my family and the company."

I glance around the table, but nobody speaks. I don't back down until I have met everyone's eyes.

Finally, one gentleman sitting to my right speaks up, "As you can see from when you entered the casino, the number of customers has increased almost threefold, which sounds great. However, we were not prepared for such an increase in customers. We don't have the staff to handle such a large number of people, and we have had several employees simply not show up to work. As a result, we have had to turn customers away."

I nod. "Has this been the same experience across all of our hotels and casinos nationwide?"

"Yes," a woman to my left says.

"Any ideas on how to solve this problem?" I ask the group.

"We have been asking our employees to do overtime to make up for those who haven't been showing up. It's the same strategy we have used in the past when employees haven't shown up, but we can't ask them to do that forever."

I nod although I didn't realize we had a problem with employees not showing up to work. "What about hiring new employees so we can fill our hotels and casinos to capacity?"

"That would work in the short-term, but when the decrease in customers returns to our old rate, we would have to lay off lots of employees."

I shake my head. "No, we won't. We can hire the same amount of employees that we will need for the expansion of the hotel, so they can stay on. Test raising our rates during this period and see if demand decreases or stays steady to help pay for the increase in employees. Let's get a marketing and PR team together to capitalize on the current situation and spin it to our favor, so the world is behind us." I can't believe the words that are coming out of my mouth, but there they are. Each word that falls from my lips makes me feel more and more confident.

"Are you sure the numbers will work? Will we make

enough profit? We can't afford to be in the negative at a time like this," the woman next to me says.

I think back to the numbers that were lying on my father's desk. I quickly calculate the risk and reward associated with the plan.

I smile. "It will work."

"What makes you so sure?"

"I just ran the numbers in my head. Even if the numbers fell off, going back to our normal rate—which wouldn't happen because we are going to increase our marketing to capitalize on the situation—we would still be in the positive. So, make it happen."

Those around the table stare back at me with obvious confusion on their faces.

"What?" I ask, looking around the table. I touch my face, afraid I have something on it since everyone is looking at me so weirdly.

"Who is in charge now that Mr. Felton is incapacitated? Or will he be working from his home for now?" the woman next to me asks.

"I'm in charge."

"You?" she asks.

"Yes. So, when I say implement the plan I just told you, you need to do it."

I look around the table at everyone's stunned expressions.

"Is this a permanent position for you or just until your grandfather chooses a new replacement?"

I glare at the man who just asked. "It's permanent." I don't want them thinking they can just walk all over me until my grandfather chooses a replacement.

"But will you be able to run the company with the charges against you?"

I turn my glare to the woman who just asked me that. "I have full faith the charges against me, as well as the charges against my grandfather, will be dropped soon. There is no merit to the charges."

"But what if—"

I glare at the woman. "If, nothing. I will not be discussing the charges against me or my grandfather any further. It isn't a concern for the company. We always have what is best for the company at heart. That isn't going to change, no matter what happens.

"Now, do any of you have further questions about the company or what our focus should be in the upcoming months?"

I look around the room as everyone shakes their head.

"Good. If anyone has any questions, please contact me or Tony. He will be my assistant and will get any questions you have to me. Understood?"

I smile as I look around the room, and everyone nods.

I can do this, I think. *I can run a company.* I just need a little confidence and a little more practice. *I can do this.*

11
———

KILLIAN

A SENSE of calm washes over me as I walk into the Felton Grand casino. I shouldn't feel this way, walking into a place I'm helping to destroy. I shouldn't feel like I'm walking into my home.

I walk through the casino to the door that says *Employees Only*. I swipe my employee card, and it still works. I open the door.

I shouldn't be here.

I shouldn't be doing this.

Kinsley might not even be here, but I have to see her. I have to try one more time.

I walk down the hallway to Robert's office. I grab the door handle, but it's locked. I knock, but no one answers, and from what I can tell, it's dark inside. I walk past my old office that still looks the same. I could go in and pretend this is still my life. That I get to feel important and useful, helping to build a company, instead of feeling like a fraud FBI agent. I rest my hand on the handle of my office door, ready to go inside, when I hear the door to the meeting room open.

I watch as several of the other execs file out of the room. I nod at them as they walk by with shocked, wide-eyed expressions on each of their faces. I wait until the last one has passed, and that's when I see her.

Kinsley closes the door behind her as she takes a deep breath with a large smile on her face. I can't help but smile at her, too. Whatever happened in there happened because she finally found herself. She found the piece of confidence that was dampened years ago. She looks beautiful and strong, standing there in her business suit.

Kinsley tucks a strand of her long blonde hair behind her ear as she looks up and straight into my eyes. She freezes when she sees me, not sure what to do, and then she narrows her eyes at me, like she's not sure if I am really here.

She begins walking down the hallway, her eyes now looking at the floor instead of me, but I can't keep mine off of her. Despite staring down, she struts down the hallway like she owns the place. When she gets to me, I plan on stopping her and dragging her inside my office, but she stops and looks at me, and I freeze. I try to read her face, but I can't.

She raises her eyebrows at me.

"We need to talk," I say.

She doesn't hesitate like she usually does. She doesn't say maybe. "No."

And then she's walking again, and I have to resort to my original plan.

"It wasn't a question." I pull her into my old office and quickly shut the door behind me.

She glares at me, but it looks more cute than menacing. "I want your employee access card back." She holds out her hand waiting for me to give her the card.

I shake my head and get straight to the point. "Take the plea deal."

"If that's why you came here, then you are wasting your time and mine. I have a lot of work to do. After we found out that the man we'd thought could run the company is a lying scumbag, a lot of work has been left to me to do." She folds her arms across her chest.

I smile. She deserves to run the company. But it will ruin her. Her legally running the company will make her look guilty. She will end up in prison.

The smile drops from my lips. "You're running the company now?"

"Yes, I'm running the company." She scowls at me. "I'm a fast learner. I can do this."

I run my hand through my hair, frustrated that I keep screwing this up, but I can't tell her the truth. "I know you can run the company. That's not what I'm worried about."

I begin pacing the room, trying to think of what I can tell her that will change her mind. When I turn back, all I see is her getting more and more annoyed with me.

"What do you know?" I ask, hoping she will say enough so I can tell her the truth. If I can tell her everything, then she might listen to me.

But she stares back at me with a blank expression. She cocks her head to one side. "What do I know about what?"

I shake my head. This is a bad idea. I turn to pace again, but she reaches her hand out and touches my arm. I freeze at her touch as it electrifies my body. I don't know what it is about her that affects me like this. There is nothing sexual about her touch. It's not even that comforting. I'm not even sure she realizes she is touching my arm.

"Take the plea. If not for you, do it for *me*."

She scrunches her nose. "I'm not going to help you lock Granddad away."

"You won't. You don't know anything that could worsen his case. Just don't make me testify against you. Don't make me hurt you, princess."

She lets go of my arm. "You can't hurt me, *Liam*. I didn't do anything wrong."

I hate hearing the name *Liam* coming out of her mouth. "I can hurt you though. I could send you to jail with my testimony."

"It would be a lie."

I shake my head. "It wouldn't be."

"Then, tell me what you saw. What evidence do you think you have against me? Tell me what you think I did?"

"I don't think you did anything, but with what I saw, the FBI will make the jury believe you knew what you were doing." I can't tell her more though. "You just have to trust me."

"I can't, Liam, not after you lied to me."

"Take the plea deal. Choose your own freedom."

"Tell me the truth, and maybe I will."

I eye her suspiciously, trying to decide if she would change her mind if I told her. I've studied everything about this girl for five years, from afar and up close. She's too loyal to her family, no matter the cost.

"You won't. Even if I told you the truth."

"Maybe, maybe not. It depends on what the truth is."

"You won't."

"Try me. Let me make up my own mind." She steps forward in a challenging manner until her body presses against mine.

I try not to show her how much her body affects me, but it's a useless endeavor. My eyes fill with need, and my body aches for her, to kiss her and own her body until she forgets why she hates me.

"Trust me," I say.

"I can't."

I close my eyes in defeat. I hear her phone buzzing in her pocket and watch as she pulls it out and glances at her screen.

"It's my lawyer," she says.

"Take it." I nod toward her phone. I lean forward and softly kiss her on the cheek because I need to touch her skin. And then I walk toward the door.

I know this is the last time we will be in the same room without her hating me. She thinks she hates me now, but she doesn't know what hating me really feels like. After I testify against her and her grandfather, she will detest me.

"My name's not Liam. I haven't been Liam since I was seven. I'm Killian. I didn't lie about that."

Kinsley smiles at me, and it's a memory I will take with me forever, a last piece of happiness she gave to me. And then I leave her to find out how long she has left before her life changes forever.

12

KINSLEY

KILLIAN CAME to see me again. Each time I see him, it gets harder and harder to tell him good-bye. Each time, it gets harder and harder to tell him no when his body is asking for more.

I walk over to my closet and pull out the pastel-pink jacket I've chosen to wear with my khaki dress pants. My lawyer said appearance is important in court. I'm supposed to look professional but not too professional. Pretty but not too pretty. He said the most important was to look young and naive, not like a sharp businesswoman.

That's not hard for me. Young, naive, and pretty is what everyone thinks of me on a normal day.

I slip the jacket on and take a deep breath, trying to calm myself, but it's no use. Granddad still isn't well enough to leave the house. My mother is still in rehab. Scarlett and I haven't made up yet. I have no one to go to court with. No one to lean on for support. I'm on my own.

I grab my purse and head downstairs.

"Would you like any breakfast?" Paige asks when I walk past the kitchen.

I stop, and my stomach growls. She smiles at me.

"I don't know," I say because I have no idea if I could stomach any food right now.

"I'll make you a smoothie so you can sip it on your way."

"Thanks."

The doorbell rings, and I stare at her in confusion. "Are we expecting anyone?"

She shakes her head and then goes to gather ingredients to make the smoothie. I sigh and walk to the door. I don't want to deal with anybody today. I just want to go to court and then climb back into bed and cry.

I open the door, and my mouth falls open.

"Hi, Kins," Scarlett says hesitantly.

"Hi," I breathe back.

"I, uh...I came here...I mean, I just thought..."

I take in Scarlett's appearance of heels, a black skirt, and a white blouse. I smile.

"Thank you," I say.

She smiles back at me, and that's all it takes to make up. We don't need any other words. We don't need to say we are sorry.

Scarlett wraps her arms around me, and I can finally breathe. It's exactly what I needed. Someone to support me today. To know someone will be sitting on my side of the courtroom with me. When she lets go, she grabs my hand instead.

"We've got this," she says.

I nod, unable to speak. *We've got this.*

"You ready to go?"

I nod again.

"Smoothies for two," Paige says from behind me. She hands Scarlett and me each a strawberry-banana smoothie. "Best of luck, sweetheart."

"She doesn't need luck. We've got this," Scarlett says, winking at me.

I smile as we walk to her car. I climb in the passenger seat, feeling good I don't have to drive myself.

"How's your grandfather doing?"

"He's recovering well. A therapy team comes twice a day to help him get stronger."

"That's good," she says, backing the car out of the driveway.

"Company doing well?"

"Yeah, it's doing better than ever actually."

She smiles. "There is no such thing as bad press."

I smile, too. "That's what I thought."

She hesitates before asking me the last question, the one she's dying to ask if I know Scarlett at all, "And Killian?"

I twirl my hair around my fingers. "It's over. He's going to testify against me today. I think, after hearing that, any lingering feelings I have for him will disappear."

"It's okay if they don't."

"No, it's not. I need to move on."

She nods.

"Do you want to talk about—"

"No." If I think about where we are driving, about what I'm going to have to do today, I'll lose any bit of strength I have worked so hard to get. I need to save it all for the courtroom.

"I went on an audition," Scarlett says, trying to distract me.

"Yeah? For what?"

"A horror film."

I raise my eyebrow. "Horror? Really? How did it go?"

She laughs. "It was horrible. Evidently, I make a terrible

scared face. And they said I was too pretty for horror anyway."

I laugh a little, too. "I can't imagine you covered in blood. You should try romance or comedy or suspense."

"Yeah, I don't think I could handle being covered in blood." Scarlett pulls into a parking spot outside the courthouse.

She turns off the ignition, but neither of us moves or looks at each other. We just breathe. In and out. Our breaths unsteady and weak.

Scarlett breaks first. "Ready?"

I look out the window at the looming building that looks fifty-plus years old. I look at the blue sky. The weather today is beautiful and perfect.

I didn't do anything wrong. Granddad didn't do anything wrong. Dad didn't do anything wrong. Justice always wins.

"Yeah, we've got this," I say, grabbing Scarlett's hand.

I've got this.

———

"Let's go in," my lawyer, Mr. Greene, says.

I follow him, and Scarlett holds my hand. We walk into the courtroom that is more crowded than I expected.

"Who are all these people?" Scarlett whispers to me.

I shrug. "I don't have a clue."

As I look around, I realize who the people are— reporters, agents, and others who are just curious about a high-profile case. None of them are friends or family though. Even though I don't really see any of their faces, I know none of them are on my side.

I follow my lawyer up to the table at the front, a table I

never imagined I would ever have to sit behind. Scarlett squeezes me again to try to comfort me, but it doesn't help. I can see the worried look on her face.

"I'll be sitting right behind you."

"Thanks, Scar."

She smiles, and then true to her word, she takes a seat at the bench behind me.

My lawyer pulls a chair out for me, like we are sitting down for dinner at a nice restaurant, not like he'll be defending me in court. I take a seat, and he sits next to me. Then, he begins pulling out papers from his briefcase while I sit nervously.

I feel the sweat building under my shirt. I nervously tap my foot under the table. And then I swing my leg. And then I tap again. I switch back and forth, trying anything to calm myself, but it's useless.

Mr. Greene leans over to me. "It's normal to feel nervous and scared. You shouldn't be here after all, but just make sure you don't look guilty. Just be as natural as you can."

I nod.

"All rise," a woman says.

I stand next to my lawyer as everyone else in the room also stands. I watch as a judge and jury file into the room, and then we all take our seats.

I see the judge's lips moving, but I don't hear the words. I'm too busy tapping my foot again to listen. I watch the prosecutor stand. He's older. His hair is graying, and he has wrinkles around his eyes.

He begins speaking about why we are here. That, by the end, he is going to prove my guilt. He doesn't speak to me. He talks to the jury while occasionally motioning to me. It makes it easier for me to pretend like I'm not here.

I try to picture myself sitting on the beach. When that

doesn't work, I imagine myself hiking in the mountains. Image after image goes through my head when the prosecutor speaks and then when my lawyer speaks. Their words don't matter. I don't have to respond to them. I won't have to testify until next week—if at all, depending on how today goes. So, I just try to forget I'm here. It's all I can do.

"Agent Byrne will take the stand now."

When I hear Killian's name, I can't help but listen. I keep my eyes forward though as Killian makes his way into the courtroom. I don't look at him until I watch him climb up into the witness box next to the judge. He only glances at me for a second, but it's enough. Enough to calm me and excite me at the same time, and then his eyes go right back to the prosecutor.

"Can you explain your relationship with Ms. Felton?"

Killian looks to the jury. "I was an undercover agent for five years at the Felton Corporation, the company her family owns and operates. I also spent time getting romantically close to Ms. Felton in order to gain her trust."

"And what was Ms. Felton's relationship with her father and grandfather?"

"She was close to them."

"Close enough that they didn't have any secrets between them?"

Killian nods. "I would guess not, but I can't be sure of that."

The prosecutor nods and walks back to his desk. He picks up a piece of paper in a plastic cover. "I would like to submit the first piece of evidence."

He places the piece of paper in front of Killian. "Can you describe for the jury what this is?"

"It's a document, a contract of sorts between the Felton Corporation and their investors, stating how much money the Felton Corporation earned during a specific time period. It's a lie the Felton Corporation presented to their investors to get them to invest more."

"Whose signatures are at the bottom?"

"Robert Felton, Lee Felton, Kinsley Felton, and mine."

He nods and then passes the paper to the jury for them to inspect and then over to our table where I glance at the evidence for the first time. I look at the paper. I look at my signature at the bottom, and that's when it all comes flooding back.

I remember my father brought me in almost three years ago over my summer break. I remember signing a bunch of papers about my inheritance. It was in a room full of executives and employees watching me sign. The company was in the middle of discussing a merger, and my father couldn't take a break from the meetings. I'm sure Killian was there. He watched me sign this paper. That's what he is testifying to. That's why he thinks I will go to jail. But they are wrong. All wrong. This paper doesn't say anything about what they are suggesting. And if it did, the numbers on it must have been a mistake. We wouldn't have purposely misled anyone about our company.

The paper is taken back out of my hands quickly. Too quickly for me to really read it. All I know is, I signed it without a second thought. I used to sign everything placed in front of me without a second thought.

I watch as the prosecutor walks the paper back to Killian. "Can you confirm for everyone how you know this isn't a forgery and the signature at the bottom belongs to Kinsley Felton?"

I suck in a breath and wait for Killian to confirm what I already know—that I did sign the paper. If that paper does, in fact, seem criminal, even if it was a mistake, they could still convict me unless we find a way to prove it was a mistake. It wasn't intentionally done. They only have one piece of paper. One signature. Not a trail of documents. That's not enough to show proof of money laundering or fraud.

Killian looks at the piece of paper, and then he looks up at me. I think he's preparing me for the words that will come out of his mouth, the words that will convict me.

Then, he opens his mouth. "I can't confirm this signature is Kinsley Felton's."

The prosecutor raises his eyebrow at Killian, obviously not expecting that answer. "Are you sure you didn't witness Kinsley Felton signing this piece of paper?"

"I didn't see her sign anything."

The prosecutor walks back to his table and shuffles through some papers. When he finds what he is looking for, he says, "Your report, dated three years ago, clearly states you witnessed Kinsley Felton sign this paper. Are you telling me this report is wrong?"

"Yes. I witnessed Kinsley Felton sign something, but I wasn't sure what. At the time, I assumed it was this paper. No, I *hoped* it was because I was tired of my assignment after being undercover for three years, and I wanted evidence to release me from my duty. After thinking about it now, I realize she was signing a birthday card for her mother. As you can see from the date on the report, her mother's birthday was the next day. I believe her father or grandfather then forged her signature onto this document. I believe they couldn't convince her to go along with their criminal activities, but they wanted the company to stay in the family, so they forged her signature."

"Agent Byrne, I would like to remind you that you are

under oath. Whatever you say must be the truth, or you could go to jail if what you've said is proven to be false."

"I understand."

The prosecutor glares as Killian, but he remains calm and composed. I don't understand why he is lying for me, why he is protecting me.

"Then, I would like to call for a recess," the prosecutor says.

My lawyer stands up. "Your honor, I would like to call for the charges to be dismissed against my client. The prosecutor has no evidence against my client other than a forged signature. They don't have any other evidence or witnesses to call."

The judge turns his attention to the prosecutor. "Is that true?"

"Yes, your honor, but we would like more time to reexamine our evidence. We still believe Kinsley Felton is guilty."

"For the time being, if you are not prepared to continue now with this trial, then I have no choice but to dismiss the charges against Kinsley Felton. Ms. Felton, you are free to go."

13

KINSLEY

I HAVE no idea what just happened, but the room seems to be spinning with chaos. I turn to face Scarlett, who is smiling brightly at me. I watch as Killian steps down from the stand and is immediately scolded by the prosecution. Killian doesn't glance my way. He just walks straight down the aisle and out of the courtroom.

I begin walking down the aisle as well. I don't bother speaking to my lawyer. Scarlett tries to get my attention, but I motion that I'll be right back, and she looks at me with a knowing face.

I make it through the crowded courtroom and out into the hallway, but I don't see Killian. Instead, cameras and microphones are thrust into my face as reporters ask about how I feel now that the charges have been dismissed.

"Good," I say with a blank stare as I look out past them for Killian.

I see a group of men wearing all black suits, and I begin walking in that direction. When I walk closer, I see Killian standing next to one of them while another man is speaking harshly to him. I hide around the corner so I can hear the conversation but not be seen.

"You can forget about that promotion. In fact, expect a demotion coming your way. You're lucky I'm not firing your ass right now."

"Yes, sir," Killian says flatly.

"And if I do find clear evidence that you were flat-out lying on the stand, I will fire you and send your ass to jail. Do you hear me?"

"Yes, sir. I wasn't lying. I realized my report was wrong. After thinking about it more and getting to know the Felton family, I realized there was no way her father would allow her to sign any documents for the company. I thought back and remembered the birthday card sitting on the table."

"I don't want to hear it. Just get out of my sight and get your shit together before Lee Felton's trial."

"Yes, sir."

I watch Killian walk past me without looking at me, and I follow him. We walk past the metal detectors. We walk out the front door and down the front steps with me trailing a few feet behind him. He walks to the driver's seat of his car while I climb into the passenger seat.

"What are you doing?" Killian asks.

"I should ask you the same question."

"Get out of the car, princess." Killian grips the wheel but doesn't move to look at me.

I can't read him, and it's killing me. I have to know why the hell he risked his job for me. *Why did he lie on the stand for me?*

"No, not until you tell me why you lied."

Killian looks at me now with his dangerous, dark eyes that are hiding more than I even knew was possible to hide.

He doesn't answer me. He backs the car out of the parking spot without a word or glance in my direction. As he turns onto the street, and I realize I need to text Scarlett.

Me: Got a ride home with Killian. Thanks for coming with me today.

Scarlett: No problem. Glad the truth came out. Be careful.

Me: I will.

Scarlett: Call me later.

Now that I've done the responsible thing, I can turn my attention to Killian and get him to speak to me.

"Where are you taking me?" I look around, trying to find any clue as to where Killian is driving us.

"I'm not taking you anywhere. I'm driving home. You are stealing a ride."

I frown. After what he just did for me, I thought it meant something. I thought he would open up to me and finally tell me the truth.

Killian doesn't though. He is cold as ice.

I don't try to get him to speak to me again. I just stare out the window at the buildings that pass by as Killian drives. We don't turn the radio on. We don't look at each other. We both just exist, lost in our own thoughts.

I try to figure out what just happened. Why I'm not still sitting in the courtroom, sweating and worried that I could go to jail for something that was nothing more than a mistake, and the only thing I can come up with is...

"You love me."

Killian looks at me, and I can see it in his eyes even if he can't admit it to himself.

"You love me. That's why you couldn't testify against me. That's why you risked everything to save me. You risked your job. You gave up a promotion. You risked going to jail yourself. All for me. The only explanation is that you love me."

I watch him swallow hard before his eyes drift from me back to the road, but I'm not going to take his silence any longer. I grab his head and force him to look at me, even though we are driving on a busy Las Vegas road. I'm willing to take the risk because I can't wait another second to know.

"You fell in love with me even though you weren't supposed to. You fell for the supposed criminal. Admit it. You. Love. Me."

I bite my lip, waiting for his answer that still hasn't fallen from his lips. Maybe I was wrong. Maybe I just want him to love me so badly that I see anything he does as an admittance of his love.

"You're wrong," Killian finally says as he pulls into a parking spot. He turns off the ignition.

My eyes widen at his words. It hurts more than I want to admit because, despite everything, I still know how I feel about this man. I know, because the second he protected me, the hatred I thought I felt disappeared. The hate was just part of the love I feel for him.

"I didn't lie on the stand because I love you."

I drop my eyes to my lap as I pull on the hem of my jacket. *How can I be so stupid and fall for the wrong man time and time again? I'm so incredibly stupid.*

"I lied because you are innocent, and all my testimony would have done is send an innocent woman to jail for something you weren't involved in. I told the FBI that earlier. I told them not to arrest you. They did anyway. I wasn't going to let an innocent woman go to jail."

I still can't look at him. I'm too afraid I'll cry because, as nice as his words sound, they aren't what I need to hear. "Thank you. Thank you for lying for me."

I hear him unbuckle his seat belt, and I do the same. I'll have to call a driver to come pick me up and take me back to my house.

I feel his hand on my cheek as he gently turns my face to him until he can see my eyes and the tears all but pouring down my face.

"You were also right. Even if I thought you were guilty, I would have still lied on that stand today because I love you."

His words are all it takes for the tears to pour out of my eyes, but now, they are happy tears instead of the painful ones falling before. His thumb wipes the tears from my face, and I hold his hand to my cheek for just a second longer, loving the comforting feeling it brings me.

"I love you, even though I shouldn't," he says.

I smile at him, and then I grab the nape of his neck and pull him to me, so our foreheads are touching as our eyes close. I need a moment of calm intimacy before the storm hits. With our foreheads pressed together, I can breathe in the same air that he does, and it's just what we both need. Our breathing syncs together and calms our bodies, finally relaxing, despite everything going on. We open our eyes at the same time, and the eyes looking back at me aren't filled with fear. They are filled with hope and love, matching how I feel. It's just one moment that connects us and promises a future that, seconds earlier, didn't exist.

We break at the same time, needing to further the connection to something more. Our lips collide in a heated kiss.

It is better than any I've had before. Because this kiss is with a man I love and who truly loves me back. This kiss is with a man who sacrificed his job for me. It's a make-up kiss, an I-love-you kiss, and a promise-of-a-future kiss; all rolled into one.

This kiss is what all kisses should be. Perfect.

14
———

KILLIAN

Kinsley's lips touch mine, and I lose it. I lose all my control I've been working so hard to keep in check these last few days because we can't do this, except we are and it's everything I remembered it to be.

I tangle my hand in her long hair I never thought I'd touch again as her tongue battles mine, begging me for more than I can give her while in the front seat of the car, but I don't want to break my lips away from hers to move inside my apartment. Not now that I'm kissing her again.

I'm too afraid that, if I stop, one of us will come to our senses. I will remember I'm risking my entire life to be with her. Everything I've worked hard for during the past ten years will be over if I choose her. And I'm afraid, if she stops to think for a second, she will realize that, deep down, she still hates me because, although I didn't testify against her, I will testify against her grandfather.

So, instead of letting her go, I pull her across the center console of the car and onto my lap. She squeals against my lips, but I don't let her go. I can't.

95

"God, I can't believe I'm kissing you," I say between kisses against her lips.

Kinsley tries to speak, but I prevent her with my lips until she is pulling away from me so she can speak.

I relent and lift her hair off her neck so I can kiss her exposed neck as she speaks. I feel her voice vibrate against my lips as I kiss her neck.

"I can't believe I fell for the one man I swore I wouldn't fall for." Her words turn into more of a purr as I send chills all over her body with just my lips against her neck.

I grin, seeing how much I affect her. I've always been good at turning women on, but it's different with Kinsley. When I kiss her, it doesn't just turn her on. She comes alive at my kisses, and it brings me to life in a way I haven't felt in years, a way I didn't think was possible after what I'd dealt with in my past.

I move my kisses from her neck to her earlobe. I gently nip at it and watch as she squirms in my lap, which only makes me grin wider. I love seeing her like this, relaxed and carefree, but I love seeing her naked and spread out on a bed for me more.

I grab the handle of the door and push it open before I climb out of the car with Kinsley still in my arms. She laughs as we climb out and wraps her arms around my neck, trusting me completely. She leans back down to kiss me as I shut the door with my foot.

I stop her and rub my hand down her cheek. "You still trust me, don't you? Despite everything I've done to you? Every lie that has fallen from my lips? Do you still trust me?"

I look into her gorgeous, innocent eyes. "Yes"—she smiles—"I still trust you. I must be a fool, but I do."

I smile, more in awe of her than before as I begin walking with her in my arms. "Not a fool. Just strong."

Kinsley bashfully shakes her head as her cheeks blush a light shade of pink. "I'm not strong."

"It takes a strong person to forgive and trust someone after they lied to you."

"Or a foolish one."

"Or someone who has a beautiful soul and is able to see the best in people, even when they can't see it themselves."

"I've made a lot of mistakes. Maybe that's why it makes it easier for me to forgive."

"I've made a lot of mistakes, too, but I still can't get past the forgiving myself part."

Kinsley nods, and then I'm done talking as the sun glistens off her still moist lips. I softly kiss her. I'm trying not to push things too far until we make it into my apartment, but it's no use. We can't do slow, not after it's been this long since we've been with each other.

So, instead, I force my legs to move faster so we can get to the apartment sooner, but it's not soon enough for her. Her hands reach inside my jacket, trying to push it off my body. Her hand goes to my tie, loosening it, and then she pulls it off my head and drops it onto the sandy, dry ground I am walking on.

Since she can't get my jacket off, her jacket goes next, falling to the ground, making a small dust cloud as it lands. I get her to the door of my apartment before we lose any more clothing. I couldn't stand it if anyone got to see her body but me. I couldn't fucking stand it.

I unlock the door and push inside the apartment that suddenly feels brighter and more like home from just having her in here. I walk past the kitchen and turn right before remembering my bedroom is the other way, so I turn back around.

She laughs at my inability to make my way around in my own apartment.

"I just moved in," I say, trying to explain my actions.

She moves her lips to my ear. "Or maybe I just affect you so much that you can't think." She moves her tongue around the edge of my ear.

Yep, I can't think straight when she does that. She stops and looks at me, aware that all my thoughts, other than her, have just left my brain. She smiles, satisfied with her work.

I push the door open to my bedroom that has nothing other than a king-size bed in it. It's about all that would fit in the bedroom, and I fall onto it with her in my arms. When we hit the mattress, I feel all of my worries fall away.

Kinsley doesn't waste any time as she grabs at my jacket again, wanting it off, and I'm happy to oblige. I hate wearing suits in the Las Vegas heat, and no matter how many times I wear them, I will never get used to how warm they are to wear here. I toss my jacket onto the floor, followed by my shirt.

Her eyes travel over my abs and chest, appreciating the hard work I've put in at the gym. She runs her hand over my body and then pulls at my pants. I stand and pull them off along with my underwear. I pull a condom out of my pants pocket before I toss them to the floor. I toss the condom on the bed for later. Her eyes darken in appreciation of my hard cock straining to be inside her. I can't wait to have her, but somehow, I'm undressed, and she's almost fully clothed.

She begins unbuttoning her blouse, and it gives me an idea. I grab her hand and help her stand while she curiously looks at me. I take a seat on the edge of the bed where she just was, so I'm now sitting, and she's standing.

"Undress for me."

Her eyes widen a little as she looks at me, and then she bashfully wraps her arms around me. She shakes her head. "No. I'm not wearing anything sexy. My bra and underwear are just boring and simple. It's not pretty lingerie. I just want you."

"All the more reason to strip slowly for me so I can enjoy your body, not your lingerie."

I don't know why I'm so persistent with this. Perhaps it's because I think she needs to feel confident when she sleeps with me again. It needs to feel like her decision, not mine, and I want her to realize she is strong and beautiful, no matter what is going on around her.

She takes a deep breath and then starts undoing the buttons on her shirt again.

"Look at me," I say when her eyes focus on her shirt and not on me. I can never get enough of her blue eyes that twinkle when I look into them. They are almost as incredible as her lips that are somehow always a bright shade of red.

She continues unbuttoning her shirt. When she reaches the last button, she slowly shrugs the shirt off, inch by inch, exposing more and more skin, until her plain nude bra makes her flawless skin that much more impressive.

Kinsley lets her hands travel over her body, touching every curve, until her hand reaches her pants, and I can't believe she doesn't do this with men every night because she definitely knows how to seduce a man.

My cock throbs between my legs to the point I'm not sure why I asked her to strip because I'm not sure I can wait. I move just an inch toward her, but she puts one finger up and shakes it back and forth.

"Nope. Not yet," she says.

I bite down on my fist to keep from growling in frustration like I want to.

Instead of giggling at me, like I expect her to, she turns up the seduction. She runs her tongue across her lip as she slowly, torturously unbuttons her pants. And then she slowly shimmies them down her body until all that is left is her nude thong and bra.

She slowly reaches around her back and undoes the bra letting it fall to the floor. My cock hardens for her, needing her now and unable to wait.

"I can't wait." I jump off the bed and grab her, bringing her to bed with me.

"So impatient." She runs her hand down the rough stubble on my cheek.

"I'm plenty patient. I waited three years after I saw you to have you the first time, and after waiting that long, I don't want to wait ever again."

Kinsley smiles, but her lips fall into a moan as I brush my thumb over her hardened nipple. True to my word about not being able to wait, I take her other nipple into my mouth, and am rewarded by an even louder moan. I use my tongue to drive her wild as it flicks and swirls and massages her nipple. Her hands claw at my head, firmly holding it to her breast and then trying to push me away when the sensations are too much. I suck again, and then she's pushing me onto my back before falling on top of me.

I smile and release her breast, loving the view of her on top of me. She sits up, and my view of her body increases.

I can't stop looking at her. "You're beautiful."

She tucks her strands of hair behind her ear in her adorable way, but her eyes stay intense and lust-filled as she stares down at me. I reach between her legs, pulling her thong aside so I can feel her drenched pussy.

"So wet, princess."

"Yes," she moans. "I can't wait either."

Hearing her say that pushes me to my brink of control. I grab her thong and rip it in two. I quickly slip the condom on that I had tossed on the bed, and then Kinsley is climbing on top of my cock.

"Fuck, princess," I say as she sinks her tight pussy on top of me.

I grab her hips, but she slaps my hand away. Then, she grabs ahold of my hands and slowly and deliberately slides up and down my cock.

"God, you're so sexy when you take control."

She bites her lip as she sinks back down on top of me. I lock my eyes with her beautiful sea-blue eyes, and then I meet her rhythm. I watch as she pants harder with each thrust and movement against her clit. I watch as her eyes grow darker and more intense, as they always do before she comes, until my own eyes intensify right along with hers. We both close our eyes at the overwhelming sensations, but that's not what I want. I want us to come together and to feel as close as we can. I open my eyes.

"Look at me, princess," I say.

Her eyes open, and we connect our souls, perfectly aligned and matched as we come together.

Kinsley is panting hard, most likely exhausted from being on top and from the intense orgasm. I pull out and then pull her to me, still needing to feel close to her body. I feel complete and whole with her lying on my chest.

I want to stay like this forever. I want to have this moment forever in my memory because I'm afraid it won't last. I'm terrified I will never be able to connect like this with her again. And I need to tell her exactly how I feel in case I don't get the chance again.

"I love you, princess. No matter what happens, this was the best. The best I've ever had. The closest I've ever felt to another person."

She moans against my chest, obviously seconds away from falling asleep. "I love you, too, Killian," she whispers against my chest.

I smile. "Sleep now, princess."

Tomorrow, we will figure out what we do now but not today. Today, we will sleep and fuck until there is no way to pull us apart, no matter what happens to us.

15

KINSLEY

I WAKE up with strong arms wrapped tightly around me. I open my eyes and glance around a bare room that is bare, the morning sun blinding me through the shades.

"Ow," I moan softly as I roll over to face Killian.

My whole body aches from last night. We had sex three...or four times. Each time was more carnal than the next until we no longer had any energy left to do anything but wrap our arms around each other and sleep. Each time, I felt myself falling more and more in love with this man.

A man I'm not even sure I know.

I don't know his parents' names or where he grew up. I don't know if he has any siblings. I don't know why he chose to become an FBI agent. I don't know if he truly sucks at poker. I don't even know if what he told me the other night was true. I don't know if his favorite movie is *The Hangover*. And I know he lied about his family growing up in Las Vegas. He might have even lied about not liking Justin Bieber.

All I know is how his eyes look when they watch me come, full of intense appreciation. I know how every muscle in his body flexes when he's thrusting inside me. I know he can make me come with just a touch.

And I know I have a connection with him that runs deeper than sex. A connection that caused him to protect me from going to jail and brought me here despite the consequences.

I take a deep breath, trying not to worry about what I do or don't know about Killian. I relax while I watch him sleep. He looks so happy and content, lying next to me. His breathing is steady, like he could sleep this way forever.

"What are you thinking about, princess?" he asks without opening his eyes.

I have no idea how he knew I was awake.

"Just watching you sleep."

I stroke his hair, needing to touch him, and I watch as his lips curl up at my touch. I lift my head so I can softly kiss him on the lips. Killian grabs the nape of my neck and holds the kiss for longer than I was planning, but I don't mind as he slips his tongue into my mouth, asking me for more than just a kiss. The soreness in my body immediately melts, and I feel the wetness already forming between my legs. Even though we had sex multiple times last night, I didn't get enough to satisfy my need for him, and he obviously hasn't gotten his fill either. I don't know if either of us ever will.

My stomach growls.

Killian laughs against my lips. "I guess fucking will have to wait until after I feed you."

I groan. "My stomach can wait." I wrap my hand tighter around his neck and kiss him again. "My need can't though."

He kisses me back, and I quickly lose myself in his body, but he pulls away again.

"Food first, and then sex."

I pout, which just makes him laugh again. Killian rolls out of bed before I can protest further. I stay in bed and watch his muscular body contract as he walks to the closet and comes back with a pair of sweatpants on. He has a T-shirt in his hands I don't want him to put on, along with his phone.

He tosses me the shirt though, and I smile and put it on before climbing out of bed. I watch his eyes travel over my still visible legs. Then they move up to my nipples poking through the thin fabric.

Killian runs his hand through his hair. "You should put some pants on."

I laugh and walk by him, making sure to wiggle my butt as I go into the hallway. "You're the one who is making us eat before sex. I want you to be just as tortured as I am."

Killian grabs ahold of my arm and pulls me back to him in the bedroom. "Trust me, I am." His hand goes to my neck, and he pulls me into a passionate kiss that ends way too quickly.

"Let's get out of here before I change my mind and become the worst boyfriend in history." He grabs ahold of my hand, pulling me out of the bedroom and toward his kitchen.

I smile blissfully as I follow behind him. He just said he was my boyfriend. Killian is *my boyfriend*, and maybe soon, he will be more.

Killian drops my hand when we make it into his small kitchen. He walks over to the small fridge. He opens the door, pokes his head in, and begins pulling random things out.

"Do you know how to cook?" I ask.

He shrugs. "Sort of. Not well. I haven't had much opportunity to practice since I lived in a hotel room for five years."

I nod.

"You?"

"No, I didn't get much practice either. I loved living in hotels, and when I was home, we always had a cook. Spoiled rich-girl problems."

Killian laughs. I walk over to him, and that's when I see what he is pulling out of the fridge—salmon, yogurt, some weird-looking bread. Health nut—that much he wasn't lying about.

He pops bread into the toaster and then scoops some yogurt and precooked salmon onto a plate. The toast pops up, and he puts one on each of our plates. He carries the plates over to the bar where barstools sit underneath. I take a seat at one, and he sits next to me.

I wrinkle my nose at the food in front of me, causing Killian to laugh.

"Just try it. I'll get you a cheeseburger or something for lunch later. It's all I have though, so if you want to have sex anytime soon, then eat."

That's all it takes to get me to shuffle the first few bites of yogurt into my mouth, which I assume is a safe bet. From the corner of my eye, I watch him smile at me before he digs into his own food.

We both eat in comfortable silence, and I find the food isn't that bad, although it wouldn't be my first choice. But after a night like last night, and what I plan to do with Killian today, I'm going to need my strength and energy. So, I'm going to make sure to eat every bite.

"So, what do you want to do today, princess?" Killian asks.

I give him a wicked glance. "What do you think?"

He laughs. "We have to leave the apartment at some point. I don't have enough food for you to stay here for more than a few hours."

"I don't need food to survive. Just you."

Killian's phone buzzes. He pulls it out of his pocket and frowns. "I have to take this," he says.

He doesn't look at me. He just gets up and walks back toward his bedroom, so I can't hear the phone call, which can only mean one thing. He's talking to the FBI.

I take a bite of the bread as I try to listen to him speaking in the other room, but I can't hear him. His voice is too deep, and the walls are too thick. I try to eat more, but I just end up pushing the salmon around on my plate with my fork.

I hear the door to the bedroom open again, and Killian walks back and takes his seat next to me, like nothing happened. I'm going to have to work on getting him to talk more openly with me.

"Who was that?" I ask, trying not to sound too nosy.

He doesn't answer. He doesn't have to. We both know I already know whom he spoke to.

"A trial date has been set for your grandfather. It's two months from now to give your grandfather time to recover from his heart attack."

I nod. "I guess I was hoping, after the charges against me were dropped, the same would happen for Granddad."

Killian bites his lip as he looks at me. I want to know what is going through his mind, but I don't ask.

"They want me to take my break now instead of after the trial. That way, I can come back with a clearer mind, and they can decide an appropriate punishment for my actions. I have a month off." He seems anxious. "I should really go home and see my parents. I haven't been home in five years."

"Where is home?"

"Kansas."

My mouth falls open just a little at his response. I don't know where I was expecting him to be from, but I wasn't expecting Kansas. That means he will be leaving me here for a month.

"You must miss your parents terribly."

He stares off into the distance. "Yeah, I guess I do. I don't really know how I feel."

With my fork, again, I push the food around on my plate, trying to distract myself. I try to think of a topic to get off the fact that Killian will be leaving me for a month to be with his family while I have to stay here to take care of my grandfather.

"You don't think my grandfather's trial will be canceled though? You don't think the charges will be dropped now that they know it was just a mistake?"

Killian freezes but quickly recovers as he looks down at his plate. "No."

"Why not? Granddad didn't do it. He didn't do anything wrong. He's innocent, just like I am. There was just a mix-up with numbers. That's all this is."

I watch Killian's chest rise and fall. Once, then twice, and then three times. Each breath he takes seems painful.

"What is it?"

He grabs ahold of my hands. "Princess, you're wrong."

I shake my head and laugh cautiously, trying to break the tension between us. "I'm wrong about a lot of things. You're going to have to be more specific."

"Your grandfather, your father—they did everything the FBI is accusing them of."

I shake my head. "No."

He grabs ahold of my cheeks and moves his face closer to me. "Kinsley, you have to listen to me. You have to believe me. Your father did whatever it took to keep the company afloat and make as much money as possible for his family. That included several criminal things. He lied to the IRS. He lied to investors and stole money from them. He hid money from the company and kept it for himself. I was there for five years. I was his closest employee. He was grooming me to take over. He told me everything. He showed me how to follow in his footsteps, just like his father showed him and your grandfather's father showed him."

I push his hands off my face and fall back in my chair. "You're wrong. My father wouldn't have hurt anyone. He wouldn't have stolen." I feel a tear fall down my face while my face reddens in anger because he believes a family member of mine would have done such a thing. "You're wrong," I say, my voice shaky.

"Princess..."

"Don't *princess* me. Don't lie to me." I get up from my chair and go to find clothing to put on, so I can leave.

I walk into Killian's closet and find a pair of sweatpants and a sweatshirt. I quickly put them on with tears falling down my face as I realize we will never work. He will always be with the FBI, always looking to find something my family did wrong even if there isn't anything there, and I will always be defending my family against him. I can't be with him and be loyal to my family.

I grab my clothes and phone and storm back into the living room. I find Killian standing with one hand in his pocket and the other holding a stack of papers.

He puts the papers in my hand. I look down at them in

confusion. The top paper is the paper from the courtroom. I quickly flip through the pages. They all look similar in that they have my name, my father's, and my grandfather's, and some even have Killian's name. All of the papers look familiar. They all have my signature on them. I remember signing lots of papers like this every summer when I was home. I was told it was just for my inheritance, so that's what I assume most of these are.

"Read them," he says.

"These are just my inheritance papers. They are nothing." I hold the papers up in the air.

"Read them," he insists.

"I already have."

"Kinsley, I'm so sorry this is hard for you. I hate that I'm right. I never wanted to be right."

"You're not right. My father was a good person!" I scream.

"Your father was a good person. He was also a liar and a cheat."

I can't be here anymore. I can't be with someone who would think that way about my father.

"How dare you! He trusted you. He loved you like a son."

"I loved him almost as much as I love you."

"You don't love me. If you did, you would listen to me. You would realize I'm not related to a monster." I take a deep breath, hating the next words I have to say. "We can't be together, can we?"

Killian looks at me with sad, dark eyes, but he answers automatically because he has already come to the same conclusion, "No, we can't."

I hate that he doesn't fight it. I hate that he doesn't say we will find some way to make this work. Some way to get around the fact I'm loyal to my family and he's loyal to the

FBI. He doesn't try to fight it. He thinks it's hopeless, just like me. I can't love him while I hate him. And he can't change his loyalty for me.

"I should go."

He nods, looking like a sad, hurt puppy. He walks me to the door and holds it open for me.

"Good-bye," falls from my lips. Then, I turn to leave him.

He grabs my arm, stopping me. "It doesn't change how I feel. I still love you. I never faked my feelings for you."

"I still love you, too, but that love is quickly turning into hate."

"Stay," he says in almost a whisper.

Even though he knows I can't, it still feels good to see him fighting for us, even if this is the only time he ever does it. I can't stay, and I can't bear to say good-bye to him again. So, I don't say it, but my body tells him my answer as I walk out the door.

16

KILLIAN

THE FLIGHT to Kansas City was short and easy. The flight wasn't what I was dreading. The next part is.

It's dark by the time I see the Marysville water tower come into view. I drive past it, trying to decide what to do. I could stop at my family's house, but I never called to let them know I was coming home, and I'm not ready to deal with them yet. Just coming back to this godforsaken town after five years is hard enough. I can't face my parents and the town all in one night. That leaves me only one other choice. To stay at the only hotel in town. My family's hotel.

Five minutes later I walk toward the hotel that is the only reason I got the assignment to go undercover in Las Vegas in the first place. Because I had hotel management experience.

I chuckle to myself. It might be true, but this isn't a hotel—at least, it is nothing like the hotels in Vegas. My experience helping to manage this hotel did nothing to help me with my undercover placement. It's a wonder I did as well as I did. I expected someone in the Felton Corporation to fire me during the first week. I never expected to last five years there and to uncover what I found in the process.

Chris, the manager, is asleep behind the desk when I arrive. I shake my head at his incompetence. I reach across the desk and grab one of the keys. I slide it into the machine to activate it, choosing a room by random. Guessing by the two cars in the parking lot, my odds are good I won't select an already occupied room.

I take the key up to my room and slide it in. But the red light never turns green. *Shit.*

I head back downstairs to try to fix the key. This has happened every fucking time I've stayed here. It happens to so many guests that several of them will leave the door propped open when they leave. I guess it's the small-town trust.

I make it back to the first floor when I hear him. My father is speaking to Chris. I wait in the hallway just around the corner so that neither of them can see me.

"Killian's here?" my father asks.

"Yes," Chris answers. Apparently, he was awake when I entered. "Do you want me to go get him?"

"No," my father answers immediately. "I don't care to see him. I am just stopping by to pick up the package that was dropped off earlier."

I hear Chris hand my father the package, and then shortly after, I hear the creak of the door as it opens and closes. I wait a few minutes longer before I go back behind the counter and try the key again.

I have to repeat the process two more times before I can get the damn key to work.

When I finally make my way inside the hotel room, I crash onto the bed. "I hate this godforsaken town."

———

I found it hard to sleep after having Kinsley in my arms just a night ago. *Was it really just the other night when she was lying in my arms? It feels like a lifetime ago.*

I yawn as I pull into my family's gravel driveway, and turn off the engine. I stare up at the house I grew up in and that will forever haunt my memories. The blue paint on the siding is coming off in long flakes. The house needed a new paint job long ago. Weeds are growing in the flowerbed at the side of the house, so much so I would say it's a weed-bed instead of a flowerbed. I look at the door where the same old sign has hung for fifty years. *Byrne Family*, it reads.

I climb out of the truck and leave my suitcase in the bed. I'm not sure if I'll be welcomed to stay, and I'm not sure I want to stay. I walk up the cracked sidewalk. I knock once on the door, and then I wait. I wait a long time before the door opens, and my father stands, looking at me, with the same frown and grimace that always marks his face.

"Can I come in?" I ask.

He doesn't answer. He just turns from the door and walks back inside. I push the door open and walk inside. I walk through the hallway to where my father is now sitting in the living room. Nothing has changed in any of the rooms. Not a picture on the wall or rug on the floor or furniture in the house. Nothing has changed. It still feels like death and pain in this house. Even before it happened, it wasn't a happy place to grow up in—at least, not for me.

I take a seat on the couch, opposite my father in the chair. As if I'm not here, he glances back to the TV where a baseball game is playing. It doesn't feel like I'm really here; it feels more like it's a dream than reality.

I watch the game with him in silence, hoping if enough

time passes like this, then it will somehow make it easier when we do speak. But, instead of relaxing and doing something normal with my father, I just feel more and more anxiety creeping into my body until I can't take it anymore.

"Are you going to even acknowledge that I am here?"

His response is turning up the sound on the TV.

"Dad!"

He doesn't respond.

I get up and walk over to him. I rip the remote from his hand. I turn the TV off. "Talk to me!"

He glares at me, his face reddening more and more with each second that passes. "What do you want me to say, Liam? That I forgive you? That you've made me proud? That I welcome you home with open arms?"

I wince as he calls me Liam. He never calls me Liam.

"Yes, that is exactly what I want you to say. I want you to say, *Son, I forgive you.* I want you to say that you're proud of me for the work I've done for the FBI. I just got promoted after doing such a good job with my last assignment." Maybe I shouldn't have mentioned the promotion since it has now been rescinded, but he needs to know I'm doing better.

He gets up from his chair until he is looking eye-to-eye with me. "I could never say that. All of my sons are dead." He looks at me for a second longer, walks out of the living room and down the hallway to his bedroom where I hear him close the door.

It was a mistake, coming here. I should have gone on a vacation. To Florida or Hawaii or Mexico. Anywhere warm for a couple of weeks. Anywhere but here.

I turn and storm out of the house.

I climb in my truck. I'm tempted to immediately drive all the way back to the airport right now, but I'm hungry. I haven't eaten since lunch yesterday, and I need to at least see my mother. Her car wasn't in the drive, which means she has a shift at the hospital. I'll have to wait until she gets off.

So, I drive down to the main street where I have only two options, other than fast food. The local diner and the local Chinese restaurant. I choose the Chinese, hoping there will be less people for me to run into.

As soon as I walk in, I realize I chose wrong, and I even consider walking back out before I'm spotted, but it's too late.

"Liam?" the older hostess says.

I turn and smile at her. "Hi, Mrs. Mapston. It's good to see you," I say as I lean in and give her a hug.

"It's good to see you, too, son. How long has it been? Four—"

"Five years," I say.

She nods and smiles at me, like she is trying to comfort me from something bad. "You should get in line for the buffet, or there will be nothing left if you let old Mr. Capers in line before you." She nods toward the man who has just pulled into the parking lot.

I smile at her. "Thanks."

She just winks, and I get in line for the buffet. When I've made it through without being spotted again, I sigh a little in relief as I make my way toward a table at the back where I won't be spotted.

I almost make it to the table before I hear a meek, "Killian?"

The voice might be meek, but I would know it anywhere. I was in love with that voice for almost fifteen years until Kinsley shattered those feelings.

Summer Hirst.

I turn and look at the woman who just spoke. "Hi, Summer," I say with a smile on my face.

Her face lights up just a little. "It is you."

I place my plate on the table behind me and then embrace her in a hug that lasts far longer than a hug between just friends should. When I release her, her face has brightened even more.

"Join me for lunch."

She glances at her watch. "I really shouldn't. I have a meeting in half an hour to decide if we are going to order a new MRI machine or not at the hospital."

I try to hide my disappointment. "Well, it was good seeing you, Summer."

Her lips curl to one side as she thinks for just a second. "What the hell? I'm the boss. I can be a few minutes late if I want to."

I nod as she takes a seat in the booth opposite me. She places the take-out box with her lunch on the table and opens it to begin eating.

"How have you been?" I ask before digging into my plate of food.

"Well, really well. I just got promoted to medical administrator."

"Congrats. You always were ambitious."

"What about you?"

I glance up when she tucks her long blonde hair behind her ears. That's when I see it. Something that I never realized before. She looks just like Kinsley. Both have long blonde hair. Both have slim, tall figures. Both flush a bright shade of pink whenever they feel embarrassed.

But that is where the similarities end. Summer is strong and determined. She knows exactly what she wants and goes after it.

Kinsley, on the other hand, has no idea what she wants. She's indecisive and naive.

But both women have let tragedy keep them from moving forward.

Is the similar look to Summer the only reason I am attracted to Kinsley? Is it the only reason I fell at all for her?

"Killian?"

I startle and look back at Summer. "What?"

"How have you been?"

"Good. It's always hard to come home though."

"It's hard for you to come home. It's hard for me to leave."

She glances down and moves her food around in her takeout box with her fork. I narrow my eyes at her. Maybe she's not as strong as I thought.

"Where would you go if you could leave and go anywhere?"

She shakes her head. "I can't think like that. My life is here."

"Because of your family?"

"No, because of me." She glances down at her watch. "I should go, Killian. How long are you going to be in town?"

I shrug. "I don't know. I don't plan on staying much longer."

Her eyes sadden.

"You should try for a job in a new hospital. Start a new life. I think it would be good for you."

She nervously tucks her hair behind her ear. "I can't."

"Yes, you can. You just won't."

"Maybe," she says.

And my heart stops. It stops at hearing her say the word that reminds me so much of Kinsley. And I realize how much Kinsley really means to me even though it can never happen. I wish my heart could still beat for someone like Summer, but it doesn't. My heart is completely taken by Kinsley, and there is no way to get it back.

"Are you really happy here? Driving the same streets. Having the same conversations. Going to the same two restaurants. Does that really make you happy?"

"It's safe here. That's all I need to be happy."

I frown but understand.

The only way I could ever be with Summer is to stay here. To live here. I could never do that.

It makes me wonder if I really love Kinsley if I'm not willing to give up my job for her either.

"I have to go." She stands and walks to me. Then, she softly kisses me on the cheek. "See you around," she says as she always says.

"Yeah, see you later."

After Summer leaves, I realize I can't wait to see my mom after she gets off her shift. I can't stay in this town any longer. I tried. I'm just not strong enough to stay here and face my mistakes.

I head out of the restaurant and back to the damn truck. I drive it the three blocks to the hospital. It is rather large for a hospital in this size of a town, but it also has to serve all of the surrounding towns for miles and miles. This is the only place they can go to without having to drive to Kansas City for care.

I pull into the parking lot and make my way inside the hospital. As I walk through the hospital, I know everyone is staring at me, wondering why I've returned after all these years. I ignore their stares and unsaid words and keep walking until I make my way to the hospital's emergency room.

I walk to the front desk where a woman who was a year or two younger than me in school sits behind the desk.

"Hi, Alisha. Is my mother around?"

The woman looks up at me in surprise, the same reaction I have gotten from everyone else who has seen me in town. I guess I'm not surprised they are surprised to see me since the last time anyone here saw me, I made it pretty clear that, when I left, I wouldn't be returning. I still don't know why I chose to return, other than I thought it would give me clarity. I thought my father could forgive me.

"Give me a second, and I'll see if I can find her for you," Alisha says.

"No need," I say as I look over Alisha's head.

My mother is standing in her scrubs with a pen in her hand. She doesn't wear the same shocked expression everyone else in town has given me. Instead, she looks at me with love and joy in her eyes.

"Alisha, I'll be taking my break now. Page me if you need me," my mother says.

I glance around the empty waiting room, except for one man who shows no obvious signs of illness.

My mother walks to me and embraces me in a hug. I feel tears falling from her cheeks and onto my shoulder. I hold her tighter. For the first time since I returned, I'm happy I came home, if only to make my mother happy.

When she releases me, I wipe the tears from her face.

"Come on. Let's go take a walk outside," she says.

I nod and follow her outside the hospital. I fall into step next to her as we walk the sidewalk around the hospital. The sidewalk was a fundraising venture she created in order to try to improve the health of the employees and patients of the hospital. As we walk, we don't run into anyone, despite the warm weather, so while the idea was a good one, I'm afraid it isn't being utilized in the way she imagined.

"I hoped you would come after your undercover assignment was over."

I raise my eyebrow at her. "How did you know my assignment was over?"

She smiles. "I've kept in contact with the FBI, just checking in from time to time, to ensure you were okay. Of course, they never told me what your assignment was, but they told me when it was over."

I nod. "I'm sorry I didn't contact you."

She shakes her head. "I know why you didn't."

"I wasn't even sure I should come back. Father hasn't forgiven me, and I wasn't sure if you had either."

She stops and looks me straight in the eyes while holding on to my shoulders to force me to look at her. "What happened to your brother was not your fault. How you reacted afterward was not your fault. What you choose to do with your life now does not mean I love you any less. I love you for doing what is best for you."

I look down at my mother, afraid I'm going to lose it. That I'm going to break down, crying in front of my mother because I can't handle the pain or the guilt.

"I'm sorry though. For all of it."

"Don't be sorry for living your life."

I nod, and we keep walking. I haven't seen my mother in five years. *Who knows how long it will be until I see her again?*

I can at least be honest with her about how I feel now. "I don't know what I want anymore."

"What do you mean? You don't know if you want to still work for the FBI anymore?"

I shake my head. "I still do. No, I have to, but..." *God, how do I tell my mother this?*

She knowingly smiles at me. "There's a girl."

I look at her in shock, and her smile just brightens.

"Finally, you've moved on from Summer."

I look down, trying not to meet her gaze.

"Please tell me you have moved on from Summer. That girl was never good for you."

"I thought you liked Summer?"

"I like Summer, but she's not right for you."

"Why?"

"She would have held you back, and I don't just mean physically keeping you in Kansas. She wouldn't have pushed you to go after your dreams. She wouldn't have challenged you."

I nod although I'm not sure if she's right.

"Tell me about her."

I sigh. "I can't. Not really. I don't even know how I feel about her." That's not true. I love Kinsley. I just can't. I keep walking as I rub my neck in frustration. "I can't have her. She was arrested because of me. I was investigating her and her family for the last five years. I can't...I shouldn't even be thinking about her."

"Oh, Killian"—she places her hand on my cheek —"don't deny yourself if she will make you happy."

"You don't understand, Mother. I can't. I have to choose. Either I stay with the FBI, or I pursue her and give up everything I've worked for at the FBI. I can't do both."

"Then, I guess you need to figure out what or whom you can't live without. You need to figure out if working for the FBI really makes you happy or if you are just doing it out of obligation. You need to figure out if you really love this girl."

"She hates me though. Her family is ruined because of me."

"She might hate you for that, but hate doesn't stop a

woman from loving." My mother glances at her watch. "I should get back before we get any critical patients, and I leave Alisha to handle them."

"I doubt that will happen in the middle of nowhere Kansas."

She smiles. "Glad your love for this town hasn't changed. I guess distance doesn't always make the heart grow fonder."

"I guess not, but I don't know when I'll see you again. I tried talking to Dad. I don't think he will ever forgive me, and I can't stay here any longer when I'm not even welcome in my parents' house."

"Your father is still mourning. He's not ready to forgive himself, let alone you, yet. Give him time."

"I did give him time. I gave him five years."

She smiles weakly. "Where will you go?"

"I still have most of my month left. I'll go somewhere warm to sort things out. Then, I'll be given a new under-cover assignment. I'll try to stay in contact better than last time, but it will just depend on the assignment and how long it lasts."

She nods and hugs me again. "Just make sure you invite me to your wedding, if that is the future you decide."

I laugh. "I don't think you have to worry about that."

She releases me. "Maybe not, but I won't think anything less of you if you choose this girl over the FBI."

I force my lips into a tight smile. "I love you, Mom."

"Love you, too, son."

I watch her walk back into the hospital. She might not think anything less of me if I chose a girl over the FBI, but I would. I would think less of me.

17

KINSLEY

"WE WILL NEED to do the commercial soon, Ms. Felton, to ensure we can get it going in full swing before Mr. Felton's trial starts," Catherine, our marketing director, says on the other end of the line.

"I have the perfect model to do the commercial. Leave it to me to schedule her. Schedule the shoot for tomorrow."

"Will do."

I hang up the phone and go to call Scarlett to ask her to do the commercial, but the stack of papers Killian gave me is drawing me toward them. Every second I've had them in my possession, I've been tempted to read them, but I'm too loyal to my family and my own feelings to give in. Instead, I brought them to my father's office with me and placed them on the desk where they have been tempting me ever since.

I grab the papers and place them in front of me. I don't want to read them. I don't want to know who is lying—my father or Killian. I can't stand the thought that either man is a liar. I'm not even sure if these papers will prove it either way. I just have to read them.

I flip the page and begin reading. That's when I realize

every page has my signature, my actual signature that isn't forged. I know because I was there. I signed them. I just didn't know what I was signing. I was always told the papers had to do with my inheritance. But I realize now that's not what these papers are. My father had me sign them as a way to keep his criminal activities in the family. As a way of tying them to me because he wanted to pass the company off to my future husband, to Killian, and he wanted insurance we wouldn't go to the police ourselves. That we would continue the criminal activities.

The papers are all lies my father and grandfather told the IRS, investors, and employees. Money transfers that don't show where they got the money and money that just suddenly disappeared. Every single page is a lie. A lie they told to make more money.

I drop the papers when I realize the truth and watch them scatter on the floor. Killian is right. My father and grandfather are criminals.

I expect tears to fall, except my tears are gone from crying all night because I had to say good-bye to Killian. I expect he is halfway to Kansas by now. Instead of sadness though, I feel anger. I'm angry at my family for what they have put me through, but most of all, I'm angry at my father because I thought he loved me above all else.

I shake my head. He wasn't a father. Not a real father. Real fathers don't lie to their daughters and then drag them into their criminal activities.

I swipe all the frames of the family off my father's desk and watch them fall to the floor, but it's not enough to satisfy my anger. I go to the wall and pull every picture and magazine photo of me off the wall and throw them to the floor.

And then the tears fall, as if my anger found a way to

turn them on, like a faucet. I collapse onto the couch, a couch I used to love just like my father, and I cry.

Killian was right, and he ruined my life. No, that's not fair. Killian didn't ruin my life. He just exposed it, and now, I don't think I can look at him the same way again. It doesn't change the fact he is an FBI agent who investigated my family. I'm still pissed at him.

I shake my head. I don't have a family anymore. They are all dead to me now that I know the truth.

I want Killian. But I don't know if he still wants me. I don't know if he will take me back after I didn't trust him and then called him a liar. I don't know if I can mend that, especially when I have no way to get in contact with him while he's away for a month. And I'm still the daughter of a criminal. He wouldn't risk his job for me. And even if his job is no longer at risk, he wouldn't want to date someone who could easily follow in her father's footsteps.

I glance around the room covered in papers and broken glass. The room used to hold so many good memories of me and my father, but now, it holds nothing but my broken despair. I can't stay in here.

I walk out of the office and glance down the hallway to the office doors of the other executives. Tony's office is next to this one. And then down a couple is what used to be Killian's office. I don't want to be reminded of him either. The rest of the offices in this hallway are taken, as far as I know.

I turn the other way and walk down the hallway. I glance in door after door, trying to find an empty office. I walk to the end of the hallway before I find one that's empty.

I push the door open and step inside. The office is small and feels more like a closet than an office. A desk is pushed up against the one small window with a small stationary chair pushed under the desk. There isn't room for anything more than just the desk in this office.

I smile. This office will do perfectly. There is no room for pictures or decorations that would remind me of my family. There is no room for lies or anger. There is just enough room in here for me.

I walk back to my father's office. I grab the laptop and leave all the rest. I switch the light off, and I walk out the door and lock it behind me. I don't plan on going back in there again.

I walk back to the office I've claimed and place the laptop on the desk. I take a seat at the desk and look out the window to the Las Vegas strip below. I feel calmer now that I'm in my own office. Even if it is smaller than my father's, it's my office, and I can run the company my way—that is, if I don't sell my shares and just decide to leave this godforsaken city. I'm not sure I want anything to do with my family anymore. And I don't give a shit what happens to this company. But I don't want all the people working for us to suffer because of what my father and grandfather did. So, until I decide what is best for them, I guess I'll keep running the company from here.

I take a deep breath, and then I take my cell phone out of my pocket and dial the number for Scarlett.

"Hey, Kins," she answers on the second ring.

"Hey, I need a favor."

"Anything."

"I was hoping you would say that. I need you to do a commercial for the Felton Corporation tomorrow."

"Done," Scarlett says brightly.

"Awesome. Be here at six in the morning to get in hair and makeup."

Scarlett moans when I tell her the time. She's not a morning person. "Fine. But you owe me one."

I smile. "Deal."

When I hang up, my smile is gone. I have to spend the rest of my day in meetings before I resign to spending my night alone in one of the hotel rooms upstairs because there is no way I'm going to go home and face my grandfather. I don't know if I can ever look at him again.

I'm a woman without a family. Without a boyfriend. And without a future.

18

KILLIAN

"Another drink?" a waiter says.

I lift my ball cap up to see the waiter standing at the edge of my beach recliner. The sun streams down on my face, immediately drenching me sweat not even the ocean breeze will be able to cool. Only the taste of another fruity frozen drink will be able to cool me off.

"*Sí*, another piña colada," I say, even though I would much prefer a dark whiskey or scotch. But neither of those would stand a chance at helping me cool off, not as long as I sit on the beach with the sun beating down on me.

"*Sí, señor*," the waiter says before scurrying off toward the resort.

He'll be back in several minutes with my drink, along with ones for everyone else scattered on the beach.

I wipe my brow, trying to get the sweat off of it. I can't wait for him to come back. Needing to cool off, I get up from my chair where I've been sitting all morning. It is now getting into the late morning sun, and the heat is almost unbearable. The women who were just chatting incessantly suddenly stop when they see me walking down the beach.

The blonde woman at the end blinks at me. I would usually be all over someone like her but not now. Now, I want nothing more than to spend my vacation with Kinsley in Las Vegas, not alone on a beach in Mexico. But I don't have a choice. Kinsley hates me for ruining her life, and I can't be with her and keep my job.

I run down the few feet to the ocean until I feel the cool water crashing against my legs, slowing to a walk until my shoulders are covered by the salty ocean. Then, I go underwater, and a wave crashes over me, immediately clearing my head of the blonde with the long legs and replacing it with images of Kinsley.

I picture her here, on the beach with me, wearing a bikini like she wore in the photo shoot. Her long blonde hair blowing in the breeze. Lying on a lounger with me.

I shake my head. I can't go there. I can't be with her, but I won't be able to shake her image from my mind, not even if I did something stupid, like take the blonde from the beach upstairs.

I'm fucked.

I see the waiter making his way back through the other beachgoers, heading toward my recliner, so I make my way out of the ocean and back to my lounger. This time, when the woman bats her eyes at me, I look away, trying to turn them away from me instead of drawing them in.

I take my towel and dry off my skin.

"Piña colada, *señor*," the waiter says, handing me my drink.

"*Gracias.*"

I lie back on the recliner, planning on spending the rest of my day repeating the process of soaking up the sun, drinking fruity beach drinks, and dipping into the ocean when I get too hot. All the while, I try to push Kinsley out of my head.

I sip the drink and immediately feel the liquid cool my body. I try to relax and not think about anything. About work or my family or Kinsley. I try to just think about the sun and the ocean and the drink.

I close my eyes and try to slow my breathing to the same speed as the ocean waves until I feel calm and relaxed. This is the main reason I came down to Mexico, but it's not the only reason. I don't have to worry about that reason though until later this week. Today is all about relaxing.

"*Señor!*" the waiter says just as I begin to relax.

I open my eyes in frustration. "*Sí?*"

"*Teléfono, señor.*"

I sigh and grab my towel. I follow the waiter into the lobby. This call can't be good. I shouldn't be getting a call when nobody knows where I am.

"Señor Byrne," the waiter says to the man in the lobby.

The man nods at me, grabs the phone, and hands it to me without another word.

"Hello?" I say into the phone as I glance around the crowded lobby, wishing for privacy.

"Killian, you need to get a flight back right away," Agent Bisson says.

I sigh. I should have known the FBI would know where I went. I can never really get away. I've been on duty every day for five years. You would think I could get a month's vacation without being interrupted.

"Why?"

"We moved up the trial date for Lee Felton, and we need you back to prepare your testimony. We don't want to take any chances you are going to blow it, like you did at the girl's trial."

"Wait...what? I thought I had a month off. I thought his trial wasn't for another two months."

"Things change. You know that better than anyone. Just get your ass back here."

I sigh in frustration. "Give me another week, and then I'll be home."

"Not good enough. We want you back by Thursday."

"That's tomorrow."

"Yep."

Shit. I pace back and forth.

"Just book a flight home, Byrne."

I hang up the phone, and I walk back to my room without speaking to anyone. I push the button on the elevator to get me to the top floor where my room is and wait for the elevator. The doors open and I walk in. I turn, but I'm no longer alone. The blonde from earlier joins me in the elevator.

I press the button for the top floor since I am closest to the elevator panel. I ask, "What floor?"

She smiles at me and bats her eyelashes. "Top floor, same as you."

I frown at her. I highly doubt she is on the same floor, but I don't argue with her. She can ride the elevator back down by herself when she realizes she isn't going to get anywhere with me.

The doors shut, and she waits to make her move until we're closer to the top floor. She drops her towel on the floor, which forces my eyes to look at the sudden movement. She seductively walks to me in her white bikini top and thong bottom. I notice she's wearing heels for some reason. The only reason I can think that she would be wearing heels is to seduce men in elevators.

Normally, I would jump on the chance she's offering me.

She walks until her body is just inches from mine. She smiles at me and then confidently runs her hand down my chest, like she has done this hundreds of times and has never gotten a no. I hate to disappoint her, but she is about to get her first.

I glance over to see the elevator is just two floors below the top.

I smile. She thinks I'm smiling at her. The doors open, and she holds on to my arm, like I'm her escort.

I shake my head. "Sorry, *señorita*, but I'm not interested."

I step out of the elevator and she follows me with confusion on her face, and that's when I realize she doesn't speak English very well. I'm not sure what language she does speak. Spanish? French? Russian? I don't know, and I'm not going to wait around to find out. So, instead, I guide her back to the elevator. I shake my head again and then leave her there alone to ride back down. I feel bad, but I'm sure a woman like that doesn't have any difficulty with finding a warm bed and a man to keep her comfortable at night.

I walk to my room and unlock the door with my key card in hand. I glance around the luxurious room I paid to relax in for the week, but now, I won't be spending more than one more night here. I walk to the bathroom and flip on the faucet in the large stone shower. I take off my swim trunks and hop into the shower, not waiting for the water to warm up.

The cool water is refreshing as I let it pour down my face, washing away the salt and sand from the beach along with my sweat. As I shower, I try to decide what I'm going to do because I know, as soon as I step out of this shower, I'm going to have to decide.

Do I just go back to Las Vegas tomorrow, like the FBI wants?

Do I stay here and say fuck the FBI so I can finish what I came here for?

My gut tells me to stay—at least long enough to follow this last lead. I need to find out whom her father met with here the week before he died. Once I know for sure this is a dead end, then I can go back home. Then, I will know I did the best I could as an FBI agent. Then, I will know I kept my promise to Kinsley's father.

I get out of the shower and towel off. I wrap the towel around my waist before pulling my cell phone out of the safe in the room. I walk out onto the balcony, trying to enjoy the last bit of sunlight as I make the first of two phone calls.

"Hello?" Juan says on the second ring.

"I need to meet tonight."

"That's not how this works. *Señor* Clavé will be available tomorrow night. He can't just change to tonight. He has other business and other clients he works with."

"I am no longer available tomorrow night. It's got to be tonight, or you can forget my business."

There's a long pause.

"One thirty then. We will call you to tell you the place."

I glance at my phone, seeing that it's already a quarter till one. "Just tell me now. It will take me thirty minutes to get there."

He laughs. "No, no. Not one thirty p.m. One thirty a.m."

I roll my head back and forth. It's going to be a long night if I agree to this.

"Fine."

"Done."

I end the call and then immediately call to schedule my flight for tomorrow afternoon. When that's done, I climb into bed for an afternoon nap. I'm going to need it if I'm not meeting these guys until one thirty in the morning.

I climb into the cab at one a.m. They still haven't called me back to confirm where I'm supposed to go.

"*Adónde*?" the driver asks, wanting to know where to drive me.

"Downtown."

"Downtown. More specific?"

"No, just drive me toward downtown." I assume that is where we will be doing business. In the heart of Cancún, not near the tourist hotels and resorts where I am staying.

The driver begins driving, and I hold on to my phone in frustration. I have no idea what I'm getting myself into or what Mr. Felton was doing here before he died. It doesn't make sense.

My phone rings five minutes into the drive.

"Hello."

"Tell the driver to take you to Fourth and Juárez."

The line then goes dead. I tell the driver more specific directions, and as I do, I know I'm going to regret this. I reach for my gun, making sure it's still hidden away in my pants leg. As the driver takes me further into the shadier part of town, I'm afraid I'm going to need it.

The taxi suddenly comes to a stop outside an abandoned-looking building. I read the meter and hand the driver the money.

"*Señor*, are you sure this is the correct address?"

"*Sí*," I say, stepping out of the car.

I walk toward the abandoned building, and the cab speeds off the second I'm out of the cab. All of my training as an FBI agent is telling me to run, to run fast and as far away from this building as possible, but I ignore my instincts and keep walking.

I get to the door, and then my hand reaches to push the cracked door open. It is less of a door and more of a piece of wood lying against the doorframe.

Voices stop me from entering. The voices are saying all the wrong things and confirming suspicions that, if I'm honest with myself, I have had for at least a year, possibly longer.

I was very wrong. Kinsley isn't safe. She's the furthest thing from it.

I slowly back away from the door and begin walking down the alleyway, away from the building. I couldn't go into that building without backup, and I'm not sure I can trust the FBI with the information I just heard, not if I want to keep Kinsley safe.

So, instead, I keep walking away from the building and hope I'm not followed. Not because I care about my safety. My life means nothing, but Kinsley's life means everything.

19

KINSLEY

"THAT'S A WRAP," the director says.

Scarlett walks over to me but not before she winks at the director first. If I weren't here, she would be all over him.

"Thank you so much for doing that. You looked great in the commercial."

Scarlett flips her brown locks back over her shoulder as the director walks by. "It was my pleasure." She's not looking at me.

"Come on," I say, grabbing her shoulder and oversized purse. I lead her out of the lobby of the Felton Grand hotel where the shoot took place. "Let me buy you lunch."

"But..."

I shake my head. "That man is twice our age. You are not sleeping with him."

"But he's hot," Scarlett whines.

I roll my eyes. "No."

She pouts. "Since when did you get so bossy?"

"Since I've been stuck running a multibillion-dollar company and finding a way to keep my family from ending up in jail."

Scarlett sighs. "Well, that is a depressing answer."

"Just get changed and meet me for lunch at..." I glance over at Scarlett, but she isn't listening to me.

Instead, she is flirting with some frat boys who are eyeing her boobs beneath her bikini top.

"Scarlett, go change," I say, pushing her toward the restrooms just outside of the lobby and handing her her purse where she put her clothes in.

She looks down at her bikini top and ripped jean shorts, but doesn't take her purse from me. "Why?"

"Because the restaurant won't let you eat without a shirt on."

"You own the restaurant. They will let us do whatever we want."

"Change," I say sternly, holding her purse out to her again.

Scarlett rolls her eyes at me but walks back to the lobby and over to the rack of wardrobe clothes. I watch from the hallway as she grabs a sheer tank top. She pulls the shirt on.

"Ready," she says, bouncing back over to me. She, finally, takes the purse from my hands. "Come on, bitch. I'm starving." She grabs my arm, and we walk to the Mexican restaurant in the hotel.

The restaurant is calm. Only a couple of other people are here since it's a quarter after two in the afternoon. It's not late enough for the evening crowds to start yet, so we easily get a nice booth. We take a seat, and I look over the menu.

"Can I get you two something to drink?" our waiter asks.

"I'll have a water," I say.

Scarlett's eyes widen at my order, and she shakes her head. "We will each have a grande margarita. Thanks."

"I have to go back to work after this. I don't need a buzz

when I'm dealing with figuring out how to implement the new marketing plan."

"It's exactly what you need. You need to relax. Who cares if the company goes under? Your grandfather deserves to have his company destroyed after what he did."

My mouth drops open.

"I'm sorry. I didn't mean that" Scarlett immediately says when she realizes what just came out of her mouth.

She's always been honest though, and I won't fault her for that. Not again.

"No, you're right. My grandfather doesn't deserve to make any more money off the company, but the employees here don't deserve to lose their jobs because of my grandfather."

Scarlett nods. "I guess that makes sense. It doesn't mean you have to give up your life to run a company you don't even want to run. You can hire someone else and make it their problem."

I nod as the waiter places the margaritas in front of us.

"Are you two ordering any food or just drinks?"

"Definitely food," Scarlett says, glancing at the menu. "I'll have the steak fajitas."

"I'll have the nachos," I say.

Scarlett and I hand the waiter our menus.

I glance back to Scarlett. "I just don't know what I want to do, Scarlett. I've never had to decide before. I've never even thought about it. And until I decide, I want to do a good job here."

"Have you heard from Killian?"

I take a sip of my margarita. The alcohol immediately calms my nerves. Scarlett was right. I needed this.

"No, Killian hasn't called. I don't expect him to. I told him I couldn't handle dating someone who hurt my family, but I was wrong. I don't have a family. I want him, but I think I pushed him away."

"He'll come back."

I nod. "He'll come back for my grandfather's trial, but that's exactly why he won't date me either. He can't date me and work for the FBI. They are still investigating my family."

Scarlett sucks down half of her margarita. "God, your life is so messed up. I don't know how you deal with it, Kins. The hardest decision I have to make is what clothes I'm going to wear in the morning."

I remember that life. I remember not having to decide anything, but I wasn't happy. I asked for this. I asked to run the company. I asked to make decisions about my own life. And, now that I get to do that, I've made even more of a disaster out of my life.

Our food quickly comes out and is placed in front of us, but suddenly, I'm no longer hungry as I'm faced with more choices and decisions than I ever thought was possible.

"Eat," Scarlett says when she notices I'm not eating.

I pick up a chip and force it into my mouth, but it doesn't taste good. It's not what I want.

"Forget this. I'm tired of seeing you mope. We are going out tonight."

I frown. "No, we are not. The last time we went out, I almost made a terrible decision by going home with a random guy and my father died."

"Well, that's obviously not going to happen again."

My mouth falls open a little.

"Oh God! I didn't mean to be insensitive, Kinsley. I just really think we should have a good time. I think your mind will be clearer after we go out. You'll be able to decide what you really want to do."

"Maybe."

"I'll take that as a yes."

A tear falls as I hear her say the words that Killian always says.

"Oh, honey," Scarlett says, getting up from her side of the booth.

She quickly climbs into the booth next to me. She wraps her arms around me, and I rest my head on her shoulder. She rubs my back, trying to stop the tears, but they keep coming. I glance around the restaurant because I'm sure the wait staff will notice me crying. A CEO who cries in one of her own restaurants—that's got to be a first. I don't care though. I'm tired of caring about what other people think of me. I need to cry, so I do.

"I miss him so much."

"I know, sweetie. It's not fair that you lost your father. It's okay to miss him."

I sniffle. "Him, too."

A small smile creeps up her lips. "Killian will be back. He would be crazy not to come after a hot, strong woman like you."

"But what if he doesn't?"

"Then, you go after him and don't take no as an answer."

"He's in Kansas though. That's all he told me. I don't have an address. I don't even have a city. He could be anywhere in Kansas."

Scarlett laughs. "It's not like Kansas is that big. I'm sure we could look up his family's address and find him, but he'll be back in town for your grandfather's trial. When does it start?"

"I don't know."

"What do you mean? They haven't set a date yet?"

"I'm sure they have. I just haven't spoken to Granddad

since I found out the truth. I've been sleeping at the hotel, and I hired extra staff to take care of him at home."

Scarlett looks at me, confused. "You need to go see him. You're the only family he has."

"No, I don't. He did this to me. I'm not his family. Not anymore."

Scarlett nods and holds me tighter.

"Let's go out tonight," I say.

She pulls away from me, so she can look at me in the eyes. "You sure?"

I hesitate for just a second. "Yes, I'm sure. I just want to have fun. No guys. No drama. No family. Just drinking and fun."

She nods. "Sounds perfect."

It does sound perfect. It sounds like exactly what I need.

I press the button for the elevator and wait for it to make it up to the eleventh floor where I'm staying. I pull some lip gloss out of my purse and apply it to my lips. I feel good in my skintight black dress, but I'm interested to see what Scarlett thinks of the change I made. After she left, I couldn't spend the day working on the marketing plan. I needed to spend time on me, on figuring me out. And, while I don't feel any closer, I do feel more like a woman and less like a girl.

The elevator doors open, and I step onto the empty elevator. I press the floor for the lobby where I'm meeting Scarlett before we walk over to a nearby club. The ride is long. The elevator stops on almost every floor as it goes down until it is completely full. It does make me happy to see the hotel running at full capacity and getting so much business, despite my indecisiveness with how I feel about running the company.

The doors open to the lobby, and everyone files out. I step off and smile at the passersby as I walk to the center of the lobby where Scarlett is supposed to meet me. She isn't here yet, not that it surprises me. She's probably still napping after I made her get up so early to do the commercial.

I plan on taking a seat on a bench in the lobby to wait for her when I see a family arguing with one of our managers behind the desk. I sigh. I guess I might as well make use of my time and see how I can help.

I walk over to the lobby desk with a smile on my face. In my current apparel, I'm afraid people won't take me seriously. But I'm not going to let it stop me from doing my job.

"Hello, I'm Kinsley Felton, CEO of this hotel and casino. Is there anything I can help with?" I surprise myself by saying CEO although it's technically true. *I'm the CEO.*

The man standing with his family doesn't even question me, like I expected.

"Yes, we booked a weeklong stay here over six months ago. We live in Mississippi and came here for a family vacation, but somehow, this man is saying that you lost our reservation and are booked solid."

The manager standing behind the desk frowns. "As I told you before, we didn't lose your reservation. We don't lose reservations. You will have to go—"

"No, I apologize for losing your reservation. I will get it fixed right away," I say, moving around the desk so I can access the computer.

I frown at the manager. I'll need to have a discussion with him later. He has to learn to speak politely to our customers if he wants to continue working for us.

"Excuse me," I say to the manager as I take control of the computer.

I scroll through the bookings and realize the manager is correct. We are completely full. There is one room though I can give to them.

"Okay, so we are almost full, but I do have one suite available."

"We booked a single room with a rollaway bed for the kids. We don't want to pay for a suite," the man says.

I smile at him. "Not a problem. We will give you the upgrade to the suite for free as a thank-you for being so patient with us after losing your reservation. We will just need an hour to get the room clean. I'll also give you some restaurant vouchers so you can have a nice dinner while you are waiting in the meantime." I grab some vouchers for our best restaurant and hand them to the man.

"Thank you," he says in surprise with a smile on his face.

"You are welcome. I will leave you to"—I glance at the manager's name tag—"Sean, so he can take your information and bags."

I smile at them and then turn to Sean. I lean over so that only he can hear me. "Put them in the room I'm staying in and have it cleaned immediately. Have my stuff packed and put into my office. And we will have a discussion later about how to handle customers."

He nods.

I glance back to the young family. "Enjoy your stay."

They smile at me, and I hand the two young kids each a lollipop before I leave. I see Scarlett walk into the lobby just as I make my way back around the desk. I smile at her, but she doesn't see me. Her eyes continue scanning the room for me.

"Scarlett!" I holler.

She turns her head in my direction, and when she sees me, she gasps, followed by a squeal I'm afraid everyone in the hotel hears. She runs to me and grabs my now much shorter blonde hair that stops just above my shoulders.

"Oh my God! I can't believe you cut your hair. I've never seen you with anything but flowy long hair." Scarlett takes a step back and takes in the full picture of me with my new lob hairstyle. "I love it!" she squeals again. "It makes you look so much..."

"Older," I say, finishing her sentence.

I flip my hair back, loving how the lighter locks make me feel.

"Yes, and sassy," she says, smiling. "You look so grown-up now. Maybe I should try a new do."

I widen my eyes. Scarlett's hair is long and gorgeous. Sure, she could pull off a shorter hairstyle, but why should she when her current hairstyle is so perfect for her?

"Really?" I ask.

She thinks for a second. "Nah."

I giggle. "So, where are we going?"

"A new club just opened two blocks down. It's supposed to be slammin'."

I laugh at her language. "What's so slammin' about this club?"

"It's on a rooftop."

———

"Wow," I say when we make it up to the rooftop. "This is..."

"Slammin'," Scarlett says.

"That's one word for it."

Scarlett and I begin the long journey of pushing our

way through the crowd to one of the bars located in three of the corners. The fourth corner contains the stairs we just came up. The rooftop view is incredible. It has lights along the railing. The whole rooftop is just one giant dance floor. A DJ is playing loud music against one side. It's chaotic and loud, and honestly, it's exactly what I need to distract myself.

I see an opening in the crowd and push through toward the bar closest to us. Scarlett follows as people dance around us. I push my way up to the all glass bar. The bartender sees us and holds up a finger, saying he will be over in a minute. I turn to ask Scarlett what she wants to drink when I notice everyone at the bar has some sort of bright blue-colored drink that looks good. When the bartender comes over, I ask for two of them, and he tells me it's their specialty drink with vodka and fruit juices.

He quickly makes it, and I hand one of the drinks to Scarlett.

"Thanks, hon," she says. "To having fun." Scarlett raises her glass.

I raise mine and clink it with hers before taking a sip of my drink. It's good.

I take another sip and feel better already. I grab Scarlett's hand. "Let's dance."

"I love the new Kinsley," she says as we begin dancing in the crowd.

The music is loud and fun. I enjoy dancing with Scarlett. I enjoy just dancing by myself and feeling free while not having to think or talk. I get to be a normal woman going out on a Friday night.

Two more times, we repeat the process of getting drinks and dancing with each other, with ourselves, or just with the crowd around us. There are a couple of pee breaks in there as well, but mostly, we're just relaxing and having fun.

"Thanks for this," I say to Scarlett between songs.

She smiles. "Happy to help, friend."

I feel a drop of rain hit my face, and I look up just as rain begins pouring down on top of us. It's beautiful up here, seeing the rain fall from the sky as the lights from the bar shine up. When the two of them meet, it's magical.

"Wanna get out of here?" Scarlett asks as several of the people dancing begin making their way back inside the hotel.

"No, not yet."

I love the feeling of the rain falling on top of us. Scarlett and I keep dancing as the rain falls. Many of the people around stay as well. I love it and hope this never ends because, as long as I'm here, dancing, my world is good. I don't have to make any decisions here.

I hear thunder in the distance, followed by several more lightning and thunder strikes nearby. That's when they begin shutting down the bar and making everyone go back down into the hotel where it's safe from the lightning.

When we make it downstairs, there are several employees waiting with towels, handing one to each of us. I use it to wring out my hair and dry off as best as I can. Scarlett does the same before we give the towels to another employee who is collecting them.

"Ready to head home, or should we try another club?" Scarlett asks.

The sound of the slot machines in the casino draws me in. "Actually, I want to..."

Scarlett sees me eyeing the casino. "Get in a game of blackjack?"

I nod.

She sighs. I know casino games are not her thing. Her eyes instead follow a group of men who were dancing up on the rooftop earlier.

"Go with them. I just want to get a game or two in, and then I'll head back." Although, I don't know where I'm staying tonight since I gave up my hotel room and I don't want to stay at home.

She glances from the men and then back to me. "Are you sure?"

"Go," I say, waving her on.

She doesn't hesitate again. She struts up to them, and within seconds, she is welcomed into their group.

I run my hand through my short hair to get the wet strands off my face, and then I make my way in. The lights and sounds welcome me into the casino that I haven't been in before, despite trying out most of the casinos on the strip. It's smaller and older than the one in our hotel at the Felton Grand. There are only a fourth of the number of tables and only half of the number of slots. This casino is themed like a beach. It's simple and consistent throughout the casino.

I slowly walk through until I find an open blackjack table and take a seat. Two men about my age sit on the other end across from me. I quickly fall into the rhythm of the game almost automatically. Even when the men across from me try to draw me into polite conversation, I'm still able to count the cards and keep track of the running total.

I win more times than I lose, but it's not the winning or losing that makes the game enjoyable for me. It's the weird enjoyment I get from being around people while not actually having to talk with them. It's the sounds of the slots mixed with the quiet intensity of those playing the table games. It's the flashing lights that energize me. It's the subtle smell of alcohol and cigarettes. Even though this side of the casino is a nonsmoking section, it still lingers in the air. It's my father.

I bite my lip in frustration, knowing that at least half of the reason I love casinos so much is because of him, but now, that reason is gone. But there are still enough reasons left to make me enjoy this, and as difficult of a journey as it's going to be, running the company, I'm not sure I can give it up—at least, not yet.

I sit here for a while longer, playing more and winning more. I sip the same wine Killian ordered for me the first time we officially met. I feel my eyes begin to grow heavy after a while, and I pull my phone out of my purse to see what time it is, but it's dead. I frown and look around the casino, but I know it's no use. Casinos don't keep clocks or have windows. It helps to keep people playing the games if they don't know what time it is.

I could ask the other players, but there is no one left at the table, except for me, and the dealer isn't wearing a watch.

I ask anyway, hoping she has a phone hidden away in her pocket, "What time is it?"

"It's one fifteen," Killian says from behind me.

20
_____

KILLIAN

Kinsley sucks in a breath at my unexpected voice. I smile, glad I still affect her like this because she still affects me. She stands and turns to face me, and that's when I get a good look at her much shorter locks. She would have been unrecognizable from the back if I hadn't run into Scarlett and she hadn't told me where Kinsley was.

I suck in a breath at the sight of her dripping short locks.

"What are you doing here?"

I reach out, not being able to stand not touching her any longer.

"I thought I would try something shorter. I've had long hair all my life," she rambles in a nervous voice, which just makes me smile brighter at her.

"Beautiful," I say because she is. She's even more beautiful than she was before. "Strong and beautiful."

She smiles, and a flush forms on her cheeks.

"God, I want you so bad," I say, my eyes traveling over her dress, her curves, and then back to her bright blue eyes. "But there is so much to say, and you still hate me."

Kinsley bites her lip. "I used to hate you. Now, I realize who I should be hating."

I stick my hands in my pockets to keep me from doing something stupid. "And now?"

"Now, I sorta love you."

I grin and do something stupid. Despite trying as hard as I can to keep my hands firmly in my pockets, they fly out and grab Kinsley. One hand tangles in her newly cut hair, still wet from being out in the rain too long. The other wraps around her waist where I can see her skin through the see-through portion of her dress, but I can't touch it. My lips touch her soft lips while my tongue tangles with hers in a desperate kiss. A kiss I was afraid I would never get again.

I thought she would still hate me. I thought she wouldn't believe me, but somehow, she does. Now, I just have to protect her from the truth I just discovered. A truth that is a million times more hideous than what either of us knew to be true.

But, before I figure out how to protect her, I have to have her. I can't stand that I left her when she wasn't safe. I can't stand that I left her feeling like I didn't love her. I can't stand that I hurt her. And I can't stand that, within a minute of seeing her, my cock isn't already buried inside her because I need to feel close to her. I need to forget what I just learned. I need to forget that, if I choose to be with her past tonight, I'll be jeopardizing a career that I've worked my ass off for.

"Excuse me, ma'am. Would you like another glass of the Margaux you were drinking?" the cocktail waitress asks Kinsley.

Kinsley reluctantly pulls her lips away from me. "No, thanks."

"Sir?"

I smile, seeing that Kinsley ordered the first drink I ever got her. "No, I'm good."

Kinsley grabs her glass of wine from and finishes the last sip before handing the empty glass to the waitress. "Thank you," she says, her eyes trained on my lips.

Before the waitress even leaves, Kinsley's soft, plump lips are on mine, torturing me. I can kiss her, but I can't get what I want right now, no matter how hard I get for her. I press my cock against her stomach to show her how much I need her, and her eyes open. They are filled with need, showing me the same thing, that she needs me. Now.

I pull away, so my lips are just resting on hers. "Fuck, that look is the sexiest thing I've ever seen."

She grins. "You haven't seen sexy yet."

She grabs my hand, and then we are walking instead of kissing. I let her lead me a few feet when I tug hard on her hand until she is spinning back toward me. I grab ahold of her neck and kiss her again. She gives into the kiss as I sweep my tongue into her mouth.

She moans just a little, and then she pushes me away, laughing. "You have to stop that if you want more than just a kiss."

"What?" My eyes widen at her words.

She leans forward until her mouth is at my neck. "If you want to fuck me, you have to stop kissing me, so I can take you somewhere that is not swarming with people." And then she sucks my neck before pulling away.

I've taught her well.

She grabs my hand again, and then she's leading me off the casino floor.

I frown when she doesn't lead me to the lobby to get a room. "Where are we going? Shouldn't we head to the lobby to get a room?"

She bites her lip as she flashes me a wicked grin. "I can't wait that long. Can you?"

She cocks her head to the side, and I realize I was wrong. This is the sexiest thing I've ever seen.

She pulls on my hand again, and we are walking faster down a long hallway and then another. I have no idea how she knows where she is going, but she does. She slows when she gets to the end of a hallway, and then she pushes me into a restroom.

I grin. "You naughty girl."

Her tongue hungrily slips inside my mouth as her arms go around my neck. It's the most desperate kiss I've ever felt from her, and I match her hunger, kiss for kiss.

"God, I want you," I say.

"Then, take me."

I lift her legs, and she jumps into my arms, wrapping her legs around my waist. I slip my hands under her dress, and I grab ahold of her bare ass.

"Fuck, you're so naughty, princess. Naughty enough to not even wear underwear," I say as I carry her to the last stall. I push her inside just in case anyone walks into the restroom.

I push her against the wall and kiss down her neck. I listen to her moans as I kiss each perfect spot on her skin.

"I've missed you so much, Killian."

I kiss her neck again.

"I know it's only been a couple of days since I last saw you, but it seemed like years. Each day, I wasn't sure if I would ever get you back," she moans.

I move back to her lips, kissing and sucking. I pull her bottom lip into my mouth and gently bite down before slowly letting it go. "I could never stay away from you."

"Good," she says just before she grabs my cock over my pants.

"Fuck," I moan.

"I missed your cock."

I raise my eyebrow. "Just my cock?"

She smiles. "I missed you, too."

She rubs my cock again, and I lose it. I can't wait a second longer. I can't breathe if I'm not buried inside her.

Kinsley must agree because she pulls at my pants to unbutton my jeans. I let her undo my pants as I slide one of my hands to her pussy that is already dripping with her need for me.

"You're so wet for me."

"Yes." She reaches into my pants and pulls my cock out before guiding it to her entrance. "Fuck me."

I pull a condom out of my pocket and slip it on before I push inside her and am rewarded with her moan.

She arches her head back as I push inside her and hold her ass tighter to keep her from falling. I grab her hair, pulling her to face me so I can kiss her as I fuck her. She claws at my neck as my thrusts get harder and faster. She gives up complete control to me as I fuck her. She has to since her feet are off the floor, and the only thing she can really do is hold on to me.

I thrust faster and let go of her hair to reach one hand down between her legs to her clit.

"Killian..." Her voice gets louder this time as I touch her. Loud enough I'm afraid we are going to get caught.

I consider slowing down so she can control herself, but that's not what I want. If she's giving up control to me, I want to prove her trust is warranted. I want to hear her scream my name, so everyone in this hotel knows she is mine.

I thrust inside her faster as I rub her clit in tight circles.

"Killian...I'm...going...to..." She pants harder until she explodes in a scream that is too loud to be appropriate. And then I come right after, my moan equaling hers.

I lower her to the ground just as I hear the door to the restroom open. Kinsley's face turns a bright shade of pink.

We wait as the woman who entered runs the faucet.

Kinsley looks at me and starts giggling. I put my hand over her mouth so she doesn't give us away, but that just makes her giggle even more.

Finally, after what seems like hours, the woman finally leaves. I unroll some toilet paper and clean between Kinsley's legs.

"You didn't have to do that," she says, curiously looking at me.

"Yes, I did."

I move to tuck my cock back into my pants.

"Let me."

I move my hands away and watch as she drops her head to my cock. She licks and sucks me clean.

"Careful, or we will never get out of here," I say as I begin to get hard again at her touch.

She smiles and finishes cleaning me off with her tongue before tucking me back into my pants. She walks out of the stall, and I follow her. I grab ahold of her hand, and we walk out of the restroom.

"How did you know about this restroom?"

"I took a wild guess. All of our hotels have a restroom near the back that only employees use. I took my chances."

"You're naughtier than I thought."

She grins a smile I don't think has left her lips since I returned.

We walk back toward the casino floor, both unsure of

where to go or what to do next. The sex was about connecting, but we have so much to talk about, and I'm still not sure if we are going to wind up agreeing. I'm not sure if she's going to walk away from me again. It's a thought I can't bear to face, but I have to talk to her, so I'm going to have to face that possibility.

When we make it back to the casino floor, we just stop and look at each other, trying to decide what we do now.

"Can I sleep at your place tonight? I gave away my hotel room," Kinsley says.

My grin returns to my face. I love the words that came out of her mouth even though I don't understand why she gave away her hotel room or why she isn't staying at her home.

"Yes."

———

We don't talk on the drive to my apartment. We don't talk as we walk from the car to my apartment. And we don't talk as I hold her in my arms on the couch.

"I'm sorry," we both say at the same time.

I narrow my eyes at her as she scoots over on the couch, so we can look at each other, face-to-face. "You have nothing to be sorry about," I assure her.

"Yes, I do. You told me the truth, and I didn't believe you. I blamed you for what happened when you were just doing your job. I gave up on us."

I grab her hand to try to comfort her. "You have nothing to be sorry for. You trusted your family over a man who had lied to you before. That's one of the reasons I love you. You are so connected to your family."

"Not anymore."

I sigh. "It kills me to see you hurting. It kills me to know that I destroyed your relationship with your family."

She shakes her head. "You didn't destroy my relationship with my family. My father did."

"You shouldn't hate your father. He loved you."

"Yeah, he loved me so much that he lied to me."

I sigh again. "It's going to take a lot of time for you to forgive your father. Just give it time." I realize I'm repeating the words my mother said to me about my father.

"Maybe."

I take a deep breath before I say the next part, the hard part. "There's more, Kinsley. More I just found out."

"What do you mean, there's more?" she asks, dropping my hand.

I look away, unable to hold her gaze as I further destroy her world.

"Whatever it is, just tell me. It can't be worse than finding out my father and Granddad are frauds and money launderers," she says in a joking manner, trying to make light of the situation.

I slowly look at her as I press my lips together.

She sucks in a breath. "It's that bad, huh?"

I nod and take her hand in mine again. "You're not safe here."

She sits back. "What?"

"You're not safe. Your father and grandfather weren't just involved in money laundering and fraud. They were involved in something more."

She bites her lip but doesn't speak. That's when I realize I can't tell her everything I know. It would just be putting her in more danger. I just need to tell her enough, so she knows it's not safe here.

"While I was away, I went to Mexico. Your father went to

Cancún, alone, on a business trip the week before he died. I decided to check it out to see where it might lead. When I got there, what I found…"

"What did you find?"

I shake my head, and I decide to lie, to give her just enough of the truth so she will listen to me. "Drugs. Guns. I don't know yet why your father agreed to meet with criminals. I don't know if he was working with them or if he even knew who he was doing business with, but those people aren't safe," I say, my voice speeding up as I talk.

She closes her eyes and then slowly opens them. "It's a lot to take in, knowing that my father might have been involved in worse than what I already know. I'm just having a hard time accepting it."

I nod. I try to give her space, but I can't, not when I see her struggling so much with this. I pull her close to me until she is lying back on my chest.

"I don't want you going anywhere alone. Either I go with you, or you hire security. Understand?"

She nods but doesn't say anything.

"Good."

At least I know she will be safe until I can figure out how to keep her safe permanently. I just don't know if that means going to the FBI with what I have, even if that indicts her grandfather or her in further crimes.

Do I gather more evidence first before I tip the FBI off? Or do I just try to convince Kinsley to get as far away from here as possible?

Right now, all I have to think about is that she is safe.

I hold her tighter against my chest.

"I have to know the truth," she says suddenly. She doesn't move from my chest.

"You will. But let me or the FBI investigate. Don't go

searching for information on your own. It's too dangerous. Promise me?"

"I'm not talking about investigating. I just want to hear the truth from Granddad. He owes me that much."

"I don't think he will tell you anything if he hasn't even admitted to the money laundering and fraud."

"Maybe, but I need to hear whatever he'll tell me. He needs to explain why. It's the only way I'll be able to move on from them."

I hold her tighter. We don't talk for a long time. I just lie here and listen to her breaths until they're steady. Then, I pick her up and carry her to my bed. I wrap my arms around her, and I promise her I will never let her go.

21

KINSLEY

I WAKE up in Killian's arms, feeling more exhausted than when I went to sleep. Finding out that there are worse things my family has done took all of my remaining energy away. And listening to Killian lie to me again last night almost destroyed me. I knew he was lying.

Everything about him changes when he lies. His speech gets faster, and his eyes dart away from me as he lies. And he was lying last night. I just don't know about what part or why he would lie.

I want to go talk to Granddad today. I need to know what the hell is going on, and I need to hear it from him. Then, I can decide what I'm going to do with my life. All I know is that I want it to involve Killian, but every time I begin to trust him, he lies to me.

I roll over and look at Killian, who is snoring next to me. He's still asleep. But I can't stay in bed any longer. I'm restless and hungry. So, I get out of bed, and that's when I realize I'm still wearing my dress from last night. I go into his now familiar closet and find a pair of his shorts and a T-shirt. I change clothes and head to the kitchen.

I walk over to the small fridge and open the door. There's the same food as last time. My stomach growls, and my head hurts a little from the alcohol I drank last night. It's not going to be fixed by gross salmon and yogurt. I remember we passed a doughnut shop about two blocks from here. I grab my phone and realize it's still dead. I consider writing Killian a note to let him know where I'm going, but I can still hear him snoring in the bedroom and don't think he will wake up before I get back.

I slip on a pair of his tennis shoes, grab my purse, and head out the door. In the hot Las Vegas heat, I begin the two-block walk in the oversized shoes and clothes. I'm sweating a lot after I make my way to the doughnut shop, which just makes me wonder more about why the hell I'm living in one of the hottest places in the country. And it's not even for a good reason, like a beach.

I make it into the doughnut shop as my stomach begins to growl, which is probably why I order a dozen doughnuts instead of just three or four, like I should. I eat one of the glazed doughnuts as I carry the large box back to Killian's apartment. I open the door and—

"Where the hell have you been?" Killian asks when I walk inside.

I hold up the box of doughnuts, and he takes a deep breath, but it's obvious from his face that he was worried.

"You promised me you wouldn't go anywhere without me or security. That includes going to get breakfast that will give you diabetes in five years."

"I'm sorry."

I realize now that he wasn't lying about fearing for my safety. Whatever is going on, he is scared. I walk over to the kitchen counter and place the box of doughnuts on it. I pull out a chocolate-covered doughnut with sprinkles and bring it to him.

"Peace offering," I say.

He reluctantly takes the doughnut from me and takes a bite. His eyes roll back in his head a little as he eats it, which makes me smile. I walk back, take out an apple fritter, and begin to eat it. I take a seat on the couch, and Killian sits next to me, continuing to eat his doughnut. I wonder, if we dated for real and didn't have to worry about my family's criminal activities, if this is what every morning would be like. Contently snuggling on the couch while eating fattening doughnuts before heading back to the bedroom. I smile. I could imagine at least every Saturday starting that way. But that might never happen.

"I still want to go speak with Granddad today."

Killian frowns but nods. "I agree. That is probably where we should start before we decide if we should go to the FBI with the info I have."

"I thought you were the FBI?"

He smiles. "I am. I just haven't reported the evidence to them yet because I don't trust them to keep you safe."

I take the last bite of my doughnut and then get up to get another. "We will go after we finish breakfast."

––––––

Killian parks the car in my family's driveway and turns the ignition off. He climbs out, but I stay frozen in my seat. I can't move. If I go in there and talk to Granddad, I don't know how I will handle it. I don't know how I'll be able to control myself. I watch as Killian begins to walk toward my house and then freezes when he realizes I'm not with him.

He turns and patiently walks back to my side of the car.

He opens the door and squats in front of me so we are eye-to-eye. "You okay?"

"No."

He nods. "Just say the word, and I will get back in the car and drive you anywhere you want to go. You don't have to face your Granddad, but if you do want to face him, you don't have to do it alone."

I gently blow air out through my pursed lips. "I can do this."

He smiles. "Yes, you can, but you don't have to."

He holds his hand out to me, and I take it. He pulls me into a standing position.

We walk slowly and deliberately to my house that is full of lies. On the outside, it looks beautiful with its large expansive doors and windows covering the front. Not to mention, there are beautiful views out back, but I would trade it all right now if I could. I'd trade my privileged life, every drop of money, every piece of designer clothes, and every sports car. I would trade it all away for a family that loved me. For a family that earned their money honestly, but I guess that's easy for me to say when I grew up with all of this.

We get to the door, and I push it open and walk into my family's house. A house I was told I would someday inherit. Now, I don't care. Now, I just want to sell everything that had anything to do with my family.

"I'm going to go shower and change quickly."

Killian steps toward me with a gleam in his eyes. "Want any help?"

I smile and softly kiss him on the lips. "No. If you come with me, we'll spend the day in my room instead of talking to my grandfather."

He grins. "And what's wrong with that?"

I just shake my head. "Make yourself comfortable in the living room. Or grab a cup of coffee from the kitchen and sit out on the terrace. It is really nice out there."

He nods. "I will. I have a couple of phone calls to make while you are getting ready."

"I won't be long."

I run upstairs to the bedroom I grew up in. I begin stripping off Killian's clothes even though I love how they feel and smell. They bring me incredible comfort, as I feel closer to Killian when I wear them, but I have to change. I can't face the world in an oversized T-shirt and shorts. So, I leave them in a pile on the floor, and I walk into the shower.

I try not to think about the fact that Killian is probably outside right now, talking to the FBI. And, every time he does, I have no idea how I feel. I feel horrible that he is discussing ways to send my grandfather to jail for the rest of his life while I also feel happy that he will be brought to justice for the lives he hurt.

I let the cold water washing over me wash away my thoughts about my family. The water slowly begins to warm up. After I let the water warm me, I step out of the shower and dry off. I put on the sexiest underwear I have before I put on jeans and a simple black T-shirt. I towel-dry my hair and don't bother blow-drying it. I put a hair tie around my wrist in case I need to put my hair up later, and then I run down the stairs to check on Killian before I find Granddad.

I walk to the kitchen and find Paige standing there, cleaning the countertops.

"Good morning, Kinsley. Can I get you a cup of coffee?"

"Yes, please."

She pulls a coffee mug out of the cabinet and pours me a cup. "Killian is outside on the terrace," she says, handing me the cup. "Good pick. He's hot."

I laugh. I should formally introduce her to Scarlett. They would get along well with their same sense of humor and single-mindedness when it comes to guys.

I pick up the cup of coffee, and that's when I see which cup Paige chose. It's the one that says *World's Greatest Dad*. I hold the cup up to my lips but hesitate to drink from it, as if it would mean I believe the words on the outside of the cup. They are the furthest things from the truth. When I finally take a sip, Paige realizes her mistake.

"I'm sorry. Let me get you a new cup."

She doesn't know the reason this cup affects me so. She thinks it is because it brings up painful memories of missing my father, and it does, but it also brings up all the hatred I have for him as well.

"It's okay." I take the cup and turn to go find Killian on the terrace.

He isn't sitting in the chair, relaxing and enjoying the view and gorgeous weather out here, like I expected. Instead, he is pacing with his phone to his ear.

"I understand, sir," he says before ending the call.

I smile at him when he faces me, but he isn't smiling. I walk over and softly kiss him on the lips, but he doesn't kiss me back.

"What is it?"

"Is your grandfather here?" he asks slowly, carefully looking at me, like I know something I'm not telling him.

"I think so. I assume he's in his bedroom. He's still too weak to do much walking by myself."

Killian brushes past me, and I follow after him.

"What is it?" I ask again.

But he doesn't answer. He just keeps walking. He opens the door to the kitchen where Paige is still cleaning. She smiles at us, but it falters when she sees the look of anguish on my face at not knowing what the hell is happening.

"Is your grandfather's room this way?" Killian asks, pointing down the hallway toward his bedroom.

"Yes. You're scaring me. Tell me what's wrong."

He ignores me and runs down the hallway to Granddad's bedroom door. He pushes it open without knocking and then runs inside. I follow, but when I walk inside the room, I find Granddad is gone. I take a step back, not expecting him to be gone. I turn slowly to face Killian, making sure to look him in the eyes.

"They arrested him, didn't they? He's in prison," I ask.

I find my legs are growing weak, and I have to sit down on the bed. I didn't expect the news that my grandfather is in jail for crimes he committed to hit me so hard, but it does. It just goes to show I still love my grandfather, despite everything. I still love my family. It just makes me feel weak and makes me hate myself even more.

Killian runs his hand through his hair. "No, he's not in custody."

"Then, where is he?"

His eyes slowly and reluctantly meet mine. "He fled the country."

"How can you be sure?"

His lips tighten together. He's not going to tell me.

I close my eyes, hating the pain that comes with loving someone who lies to me and keeps things from me, but that has been my whole life.

"The FBI wants me to bring you in."

I open my eyes. "What? Why?"

"Because they think you helped get him out of the country, and if they have you in custody, they think it will compel your grandfather to return to the country."

My eyes widen when I realize Killian is going to have to choose between the FBI and me. His pained expression tells me everything. That the decision is painful instead of being simple.

His work as an FBI agent means something to him. It means as much as a relationship with me, but he can't have both, and I hate that I have to make him choose. If he chooses the FBI, I will spend my life hating him and missing him. If he chooses me, he will spend his life resenting me for making him give up his career. There is no good choice; there is no right choice. That's what I have learned; there is only the best choice among bad choices. It makes me never want to have to choose anything at all.

"What are you going to do?" My eyes meet his, and I see his need for me reflected in his eyes. But I also get a glimpse of his loyalty to the FBI.

"I don't know."

I fall back on the bed, closing my eyes. I just want to curl up in bed and go to sleep. Sleep until this is all over. Until I know for sure if Killian and I can be together. This ache, this pain at constantly being pulled together and then ripped apart, is slowly killing me. I wish I could find a way to let go of the love I feel for him. I wish I could just find a normal man who knows nothing about my family, so I could love freely without consequence. I don't get to choose who my heart falls for though.

I open my eyes and watch Killian pace back and forth in the room, like he always does when he's anxious. I shake my head. I'm not going to let him make this decision. I'm going to figure out where my grandfather is and get him to turn himself in. That's the only way Killian and I can be together —if I help the FBI.

I abruptly stand up. "Take me to the Felton Grand."

"Why?"

"If Granddad fled the country, he would have had to stop at the casino. There is a safe where my family keeps things, like passports. Maybe he left a clue as to where he went. And, if I can find him, maybe I can convince him to turn himself in."

"You don't need to do that."

"Yes, I do." I walk past Killian. "Let's go."

22

KILLIAN

WE STAND IN AN ALLEYWAY, just outside Kinsley's family's casino.

"No fucking way. You are staying here," I say.

"I'm going. You don't even know what you are looking for. I need to go."

"You are staying here. If I have to handcuff you to that pipe to keep you here, I will. You are not going inside. It's not safe. I will not have you arrested. Not again. Not until we figure out a plan."

Kinsley pouts at me, but I'm not giving in. I agree that her grandfather might have stopped here first before leaving, and if we can find him before the FBI, then we can possibly convince him to turn himself in and plead guilty, putting an end to all of this.

"Stay here. Promise me."

She looks down and then back up. I catch her gaze with my eyes.

"I'll stay. I promise," she mutters.

I blow out the breath I was holding. I'm not sure I believe her, but I'm going to have to. I don't have another choice. I'll just have to be quick so she isn't tempted to follow me.

I grab her face and plunge my tongue into her mouth. I know she is worried that I love my job more than her. That I can't give it up. She has every right to worry, but she needs to know it doesn't change how I feel about her. I love her, and the only way I can show her right now is with a kiss. So, I try to tell her everything with the kiss.

I try to pull away, but she bites my lip, holding me in place, making me want to stay, but I can't stay. I have to protect her, and the only way is to put an end to this.

I gently pull away. "I'll be right back."

Her lips pull into a tight smile, and then I walk away from her and into the casino. I look straight ahead as I walk. I don't look any employee in the eyes. I don't scan the crowd to see if there are other FBI agents here. I just look forward, hoping no one will notice I'm here. Although, if the FBI decides to pull the security camera tapes to see if Lee came back here first, they will know I was here as well, even if no one spots me.

I walk until I get to Robert's office, and then I pull the key Kinsley gave me out of my pocket. I unlock the door, and I push my way inside. And then I stand, frozen, looking at the mess of an office. It looks like someone was rummaging in here, searching for something. Papers are scattered on the ground. Frames are shattered on the floor. I walk over to the desk, and am surprised to see none of the drawers are open, making me throw out the theory someone was searching for something in here.

I bend down and pick up one of the papers off the floor. It's one of the papers I gave Kinsley. That's when I realize what this is. Kinsley did this. Her grief did this. I pick up the pile of papers that have the evidence I shouldn't have even shown Kinsley on them, and I put them into the shredder. I walk back to the desk and pick up a picture of Kinsley and her father when she was probably six or seven years old. She's sitting on his shoulders, and they look happy. They loved each other, and now, thanks to a lie, that love is broken. Just like my lies have prevented her from trusting me, her father's lies have prevented her from loving his memory.

I inspect the rest of the office, but I don't think her grandfather came in here. I walk out the door, careful to lock it behind me.

"Looking for Kinsley?" Tony says as he walks out of his own office.

"Yes," I lie.

"She moved to an office down the hall. I haven't seen her yet today, but she is usually in within the hour. You can wait for her there."

"Which room is her office?"

"The last one on the left, down that hallway," Tony says, pointing down the hallway.

"Thanks, Tony. I figured you would have been mad at me for what I did," I say.

"I am, but I still think you and Kinsley belong together. And I still think you are a good person even if you are working for the other side."

I nod and begin walking down the hallway toward her office. Kinsley didn't mention that she had moved into her own office. I guess she didn't think her grandfather would go to her office. I don't think he would have either, but I will check it out under the guise of looking for Kinsley. And, before I leave, I will have to check downstairs to see if anyone in the lobby saw him coming in.

I walk to the last door on the left and test the doorknob.

The door is unlocked. I push the door open and step inside. That's when I realize why Kinsley didn't bother locking it. There is nothing here but a desk and a cord that connects to a laptop that isn't here. Next to it is a scribbled note and an envelope.

I pick up the note and read the shaky handwriting.

To Kinsley,

I'm sorry, but I had to leave. I've gone to make things right. I couldn't put you through a trial where the FBI would bring out false evidence against me and use it to send me to jail for the rest of my life. I couldn't put you through that.

I know this is a lot for you to understand. I know you don't understand why your father and I did the things we did, but in time, I hope you understand.

I've left the company to you with no strings attached. I won't be coming back to claim any right to it. It's yours to do with as you wish although my only wish is that it stays in the family.

I'll contact you when things are safe, and we can talk.

I love you, sweetheart.

~Granddad

The envelope is also addressed to her, and I go to open it when I hear a knock on the door. I put both into my jacket pocket and turn to see who is at the door.

"Killian, I wasn't expecting to see you here. I thought you were going to look at Kinsley's house. Any sign of her yet?" Agent Liddell asks.

"No. I tried her house and then here. I was thinking of trying her friend Scarlett's house next."

He nods. "Good thinking. I have a team in place here searching for evidence and they will be on the lookout for her."

I walk past him. "I checked this room. There is nothing here."

"Do you need backup to go with you to bring in the girl?"

I smile. "No. She trusts me. I will have better luck if I go alone."

"Be careful. These people are dangerous."

I nod. "Are we sure she didn't travel with her grandfather out of the country?"

"The video surveillance of the airport just showed her grandfather, so that's all we have to go by for now."

I walk past him without saying another word.

"Agent Byrne"—I stop walking as he walks to me—"Make sure you bring her in. Your standing with the FBI depends on it."

I glare at him, and then I walk away. I know where her grandfather went. I think I had known before we came here, but now, I'm positive, and I know, even if we found him, there is no way to convince him to come back to the U.S.

I walk through the busy lobby floor but stop when I hear a deep voice that stands out in the crowd. It's the same voice I heard in Mexico. I turn to try to catch the man's face that matches the voice, but he's gone, and I have to keep walking. I have to protect Kinsley.

I only have two choices. As my heart races faster while I get closer to Kinsley, I realize it's really not a choice at all. I can either turn her over to the FBI and deal with the fact that Kinsley could end up in jail again or...

I turn the corner and find Kinsley still standing where I left her in the alleyway. She has her cell phone in her hand, and she is mindlessly scrolling through it. She stops when she sees me. I run to her.

"We are leaving the country. Right now."

23

KINSLEY

I NOD. "You found out where my grandfather is?"

"No. But it's not safe here."

I cross my arms over my chest. "I'm not leaving with you. Not until you start telling me what's going on."

He frowns. "I will tell you, but I can't tell you here. When we get somewhere safe, I will tell you."

We both hear a loud popping noise, which makes me jump. Killian jumps in front of me and pulls a gun out from his waistband I didn't even know he had. He's pointing the gun at the alleyway, but I'm no longer concerned with whatever the noise is.

"You have a gun."

He scans the area one more time, and then a slow grin forms on his face as he puts the gun back into the waist of his pants. "I'm an FBI agent. FBI agents have guns."

I nod slowly, but he pulled it out, which means, for whatever reason, he really doesn't think we are safe.

"We need to go."

I open my mouth to answer but then bite my lip.

"Trust me," he says.

I don't trust him. I know at least half of the words coming out of his mouth are lies. The problem is, if I want to find out what the truth is, I'm going to have to trust him —at least temporarily.

"Okay."

He grabs my arm, and then without another word, we are moving, not running but more than simply walking. We are moving through the strip of Las Vegas to the parking garage where his rental car is. He doesn't look at me. He doesn't speak. His eyes are intensely focused on the task at hand.

When we get to his car, he holds the door open for me, and I climb inside. He goes around to the driver's side and immediately begins driving.

"Where are we going?" I ask.

He doesn't answer. Instead, he pulls out a cell phone. "I need you to meet me at the airport in half an hour with two passports—one for me and one for the girl—plenty of cash, and a flight out of here."

I try to listen carefully to hear the other side of the conversation, but it's a useless endeavor.

"Dang it, Hayes. I am doing this to protect her."

He pauses.

"Fuck the FBI! They would just arrest her, which is as good as a death sentence."

I shake a little when he raises his voice and when he talks about me dying if I went to jail.

"I'll tell them after. We just have to get out of here right now."

He pauses.

"Don't give me that bullshit! Just get us out of here. Now!"

Killian ends the call.

I take a deep breath and ask again. "Where are we going?"

He grabs my hand. "I don't know, but let's try to relax and enjoy this. Pretend we are going on a surprise vacation somewhere."

I smile, liking the idea that I will get to spend some quality alone time with Killian, but I hate not knowing where we are going. I hate not understanding what is happening.

He parks the car in front of the airport and gets out. He is pulling me into the airport, and I have no idea how to handle this. I have no idea what's happening. All I know is, I'm trusting a man I love, despite his lies, and I have no idea if it's the worst or best decision I've ever made.

24

KILLIAN

I DRAG Kinsley into the airport while doing my best to ensure her safety. I scan crowds for faces, listen for voices, and look for anything suspicious. I scan for anything that could be used as a weapon against us. I know I've been trained as an FBI agent, but I haven't had to use any of the physical training in over five years. I've been strictly focused on investigating this family, not on using any physical combat skills. I've barely even fired a gun in five years. I feel my senses are a bit rusty when it comes to sniffing out immediate danger.

Kinsley's hand is warm and shaky as I move her into the airport terminal. I try to be her rock, to keep her calm and steady, but if I'm honest, I'm just as nervous as she is. I've been an FBI agent for ten years now, but if she knew how many times I fucked up, she wouldn't trust me so easily.

I spot Agent Hayes sitting at a table in Starbucks. He has a ball cap and shades on to make it harder to be seen on the security cameras. I'm asking a lot of him to be here. Too much even for a friend whose ass I've saved, which was the only positive thing I've done while working for the FBI. I see him, but we walk past him to the restroom. I'm not going to put him further at risk by having him being seen plainly on security tapes, handing me what I need to escape. I'm at least going to make it difficult for the FBI to convict him.

I turn to Kinsley. "Go into the restroom. Wait five minutes, and then meet me here. Understand?"

She nods and looks at me with concern, but she does what I ask without question. I think she finally realizes it's useless to ask me questions right now when I won't answer her. When we get to wherever Agent Hayes is sending us, I don't know if I'll tell her then either, but she'll have a better shot of convincing me then.

I head into the men's restroom and wait.

"Byrne?" Agent Hayes says about five seconds after I enter the restroom.

"Did you get the stuff?"

He glares at me and hands me a bag. "It's all there."

I unzip it and see the cash, passports, and tickets along with some basic clothes and toiletries to make us look more like average travelers.

"Thanks."

"We are even now. Are you sure you know what you are doing? If you do this, you will never be able to step foot in this country again without being arrested. You are risking spending your life in jail for her. Why?"

"I couldn't protect my brother. I couldn't protect Summer, but I can protect her. I can't live with myself if I don't do it."

"The FBI can protect her here if you would just tell us what's going on."

"I will tell them just as soon as she is out of the country

and safe. I don't trust them. I don't trust that they won't arrest her."

"They won't."

"I need you to do one more thing for me."

Agent Hayes glares at me. "You already got your one thing."

"I want you to run facial recognition software on the security tapes at the Felton Grand."

He narrows his eyes at me. "And what are we looking for?"

"Anyone involved in criminal activities in Mexico. I'll let you know more soon. Just do it."

He sighs and then pulls me into a quick hug. "Be safe."

And then he's gone. I walk back out of the restroom and find Kinsley waiting. She watches Agent Hayes leave, who doesn't even acknowledge she is standing there. And then she looks curiously at me.

"Let's go."

We walk quickly and efficiently through the crowd and get in line at security. I dig out our fake passports and hand one to Kinsley. "I'm Justin Briggs, and you're Megan Slade."

Her eyes widen.

"What's wrong?"

"Nothing. Just..."

I look at the passport again. "The last name."

"You know about Tristan Slade? You know what happened that night?"

"Yeah, it was the reason the FBI started investigating your family."

She looks down at her feet. "So, it is my fault."

"No." I pull her chin up so I can kiss her soft lips. "It wasn't your fault. You didn't do anything wrong."

The line moves, and we are forced to move forward,

closer to TSA. I need to make sure she understands how serious this is before we get up there, and I need to get her mind off of feeling guilty, thinking she is the reason her family was investigated in the first place.

"You need to make sure you memorize everything on the passport. You need to know your name so that, if someone says it, you answer automatically. You need to make sure you know the birthday and birthplace. You need to have a back story so that you aren't flustered if people ask."

"Megan Joy Slade. Born May 3, 1994, in San Diego, California. I just graduated with a degree in mathematics from UCLA. Before teaching high school math this fall, I'm spending some vacation time in"—she glances at her ticket —"Tokyo, Japan, with my new boyfriend, Justin Briggs, who was born September 19, 1986, in Nashville, Tennessee. You teach business class at the local community college."

I smile at how she is able to remember everything after one glance of the passports. "Wow. Impressive. You even came up with a good story. If I didn't know better, I would suspect you of being in the FBI."

"Nah, I'm not FBI. I'm CIA," she says, which makes us both laugh. Her face brightens more as a thought enters her head. "Wait...when you went undercover for the FBI at Felton Corporation, you were given a new identity, but somehow, you ended up as Killian Browne—your name with only a slight variation on the last name. You fucked up, didn't you?"

Now, I'm laughing at how she said the word *fuck*, like a five-year-old who doesn't know the real meaning.

"Yes, I fucked up. I said the wrong name the first time I met your father, and then all I could do was change my last name, which is just a small change from my actual last name."

She laughs, and it's beautiful, seeing her laugh, even if it's at my expense.

"So, what was the name you were supposed to say? What name would I have known you by if you hadn't fucked up?"

"Harry Andrews."

She wrinkles her nose and then laughs again. "That's a terrible name."

I laugh. "Well, I'm glad I said the wrong name then. You might never have gone for me if you thought my name was Harry."

We step up to the TSA agent and hand him our passports.

"Have a nice trip, Justin," the man says, handing back my passport.

"Enjoy your trip, Megan," he says to Kinsley.

I take a deep breath. One step down and a million more to go before we make it to our destination. And I won't be able to breathe normally until we make it to our final destination.

25

KINSLEY

WE HAVE cramp coach seats on the airplane. I'm sitting next to the window, and Killian is in a middle seat. A teenage girl with earbuds in is sitting in the aisle seat. I want to ask Killian what is going on, but I know he won't answer as long as she is sitting next to us, even with the earbuds on. I also don't know if he will even talk to me after she gets up since other passengers are near us. I don't think I can wait to get more answers until we get to Tokyo.

But I have to wait.

I wait almost three hours into the flight before the girl gets up and goes to the restroom.

"I need answers now," I say in a hushed voice to Killian.

"I can't tell you here," he says, glancing around the plane.

"Killian…"

He eyes me.

"I mean, Justin. I need to know. I deserve to know."

He reluctantly leans in closer to me until his lips are right at my ear. "There isn't much more to say. All I know is that your father met with drug traffickers in Mexico. I don't know if he knew who he was meeting with or what the connection was, but I don't want to wait around and possibly put your life in danger if those men thought you were ratting them out to the FBI."

He's hiding something, but I don't know what it is.

"So, what is the plan now?"

"We are going to go somewhere safe where the drug traffickers can't find us. And then I will contact the FBI to explain why I did what I did."

"And do you think the FBI is going to be okay with you harboring a fugitive? You don't think they will take your job for this?"

"I think they will understand when I explain the circumstances."

I nod although I'm not sure if he believes the words he said. He seems worried although maybe that's just because he's trying to protect me.

"Where are we going? How long will we have to stay there?"

But I realize my time is up. He's not going to answer any more of my questions as the girl takes her seat next to him.

"Sleep, princess. Let me worry about everything."

I force my lips into a tight smile, and then I lean back and close my eyes. I try to sleep, but I can't. All I can think about is everything I don't know. Everything he isn't telling me.

I glance over at Killian. He has a little drool running down his chin. I smile and wipe it off him. I snuggle into his shoulder. Even though I can't sleep, I'm glad I can at least be with him.

When we finally land in Tokyo, I'm exhausted and in need of a bed. Killian holds my hand as we get off the plane and walk through customs. I've been to Tokyo several times with my father. I love the city. I love the architecture and the food, so I'm excited to spend some time in Tokyo with Killian.

We walk out to the curb, and Killian gets a taxi. He tells the driver an address, and I yawn and lean against his shoulder, barely keeping my eyes open. We drive thirty minutes before the taxi stops outside an old abandoned building.

"I'll pay you double if you wait for us here for five minutes," Killian says.

The driver agrees, and we step out of the car. I look around at where we are, but it doesn't look like any of the hotels I have ever been to.

Killian grabs my hand. "We need to get new passports, and then we will go."

"Why do we need new passports?"

"Because I don't want anyone to have any way to track where we are."

I look into the abandoned building. "How do you know this place will be able to get us new passports? How do you know about this place?"

He frowns at my questions.

"The FBI has connections."

I sigh when that's all he says. We enter the building, but I can't see anything. It's so dark in here.

"You know how you said you wanted to protect me? I'm not sure if dragging me into an abandoned building is the best way to do that."

He laughs at that.

Lights come on, and an older Japanese man walks into the room.

"Do you have the passports?" Killian asks. I don't remember Killian calling anyone on the plane, but he must have when he went to the restroom or when I dozed off.

The man nods and hands him the passports.

Killian walks over to him and pulls out some cash to hand to the man. He inspects the passports and then nods his thank-you.

"Let's go," Killian says to me.

"Where to?"

"Airport," is all he says.

I sigh as he leads me back to the taxi. He hands me the passport, which I study. I am now Erin Buffet. I glance at Killian's that reads Scott Foss. I lean my head back on Killian's shoulder and try to sleep. *Who knows when I'll get to sleep in a bed?*

26

KINSLEY

WE HAVE BEEN FLYING for more than thirty-six hours now. I haven't slept in over forty-eight hours. My eyes are red and dry. My back aches from sitting in cramp plane chairs. I'm exhausted. We have been to Tokyo, Berlin, Paris, London, and now Dublin. I have no idea when we are finally going to settle somewhere or if this is my life now.

"When's our next flight?" I ask as we get off the plane.

"We are here," Killian says, smiling.

"Oh, thank God," I say, which just makes him smile brighter.

He grabs ahold of my hand as we walk through customs in the busy airport.

"Are we staying in Dublin?"

"No."

I want to ask him where then, but I'm tired of getting ignored. If he ignores me one more time, I swear, I'm going to lose it, so I'll be patient until we get to wherever we are going. Then, when we are safe, I'll ask all the questions he promised he would answer.

I follow Killian onto a bus, but it is no more helpful in

telling me where we are going since there are a billion stops on this bus route, according to the man we bought our tickets from at the ticket counter. I take a seat, and Killian sits next to me. He immediately puts his arms around me so I can rest my head on his shoulder and try to sleep.

"Are we Erin and Scott here, or Killian and Kinsley?"

He sighs and kisses me on the forehead. "Erin and Scott."

I nod sadly. I'm tired of being Erin and Scott although I already answer to the name. I don't like Erin. Erin is tired and grumpy and hungry all the time. Erin wears crappy clothes and doesn't do her makeup. Erin doesn't have a future. If I think too much about it though, Kinsley didn't have much of a future either.

"Just sleep, princess. We still have a couple of hours' drive ahead of us."

I sigh in frustration and close my eyes, but I don't sleep. Instead, about twenty minutes into the ride, I open my eyes and look out at the green countryside as it passes by. It's beautiful here. There are rolling hills covered in green grass with an occasional herd of sheep or goats. I glance up and notice Killian has his head rested on mine and is sound asleep. I envy him. He's been able to sleep on every plane ride and now bus ride while I haven't slept an ounce yet.

I continue to watch the beautiful countryside as we drive down the curvy roads. About an hour into the ride, it begins to rain, which somehow makes the landscape even more beautiful, but unlike everyone else on the bus, it still doesn't put me to sleep. So, instead, I count the raindrops on the window.

About two and a half hours into the ride, the bus driver comes to a stop outside of a city called Galway.

"This is us," Killian says, grabbing our one bag that only

has one spare item of clothing for each of us but is mostly filled with cash.

I don't know what we are supposed to do when we run out of cash.

We step off of the bus and out into the rain.

"This way," Killian says, taking my hand and leading me down a city street.

I shiver a little as the rain pelts down on top of me. We walk for twenty minutes in the cold rain until I can't take it any longer.

"Where the fuck are we going? I'm exhausted. I'm hungry. I'm wet and not in a good way. And, I swear, we already passed that same pub ten minutes ago. If you don't find us a place to sleep in the next five minutes, I swear, I'm going home. I don't care if it's safe or not."

Killian's mouth falls open a little at my words. "I'm sorry. I have a cousin who lives around here. I thought we could just stay with him, but..."

"You are clearly lost, so let's just see if that bed-and-breakfast back there has any availability tonight, and we can try again tomorrow."

I begin walking in that direction without waiting to see if Killian agrees or not. It's a freaking bed-and-breakfast, for goodness' sake. It's about as safe a place as you can get. Plus, if anybody followed us and took that crazy schedule, there is no way in hell they have enough energy to come after us tonight.

So, I walk, and Killian follows me. Within five minutes, we are being escorted to our gorgeous room in the bed-and-breakfast. I open the door to our room, and it's fantastic. A huge white canopy bed sits in the center of the room with a few blue and green accents scattered throughout the room. There is a balcony leading out to the city street below and a large bathroom off the room. I don't care about all of that though. All I care about is the bed. I immediately walk over to it and crash onto it.

I blow out a breath as my body sinks into the heavenly bed. "You have to come try this bed. It's amazing."

Killian walks over to me and leans down so his mouth hovers over my ear. "I have some phone calls to make."

I frown.

"You sleep. I'll make some phone calls, and then I'll join you in a few minutes. I'm going to be out in the hallway if you need me, okay?"

I nod although it's not okay. After the trip we have had, I want his arms wrapped around me. I want to feel his warm breath on my neck as he softly kisses me until I fall asleep. I don't want to be alone, but I don't tell him any of that. I let him kiss me on the cheek. Then, he walks back out the door while I do my best to sleep alone in a strange place, in a strange country, and I still don't know what or who we are running from.

I'll ask him tomorrow, I promise myself. Tonight, I need to sleep.

———

I wake up the next morning and roll over, expecting to see a sleeping Killian. Instead, I find an empty bed and a note.

Morning, princess.

Went to find my cousin, so we will have a place to stay on a more permanent basis. They have doughnuts downstairs for breakfast, so you should be good until I get back. Don't leave the bed-and-breakfast. Be back soon.

~K

I crumble the note and toss it toward the trash can in

the corner of the room. I miss, and I watch it bounce once on the floor before coming to a stop. I hate his note.

I look at the clock that says it's almost eleven a.m., and Killian still isn't back yet, although I don't know how long he's been gone. I get out of bed and realize I'm still wearing the same clothes I was last night. I walk over to the corner of the room where Killian laid out my clothes but took the bag, leaving me with no money, no ID, nothing.

He left me stranded.

I take a shower, and then I change into the new clothes, which consists of a pair of jeans that's a size or two too big and a white cotton T-shirt. I don't look great in them, but at least I am clean.

I head downstairs, but I am guessing that whatever breakfast was served is now long over.

"Good morning," one of the owners says when I make it to the lobby.

"Good morning. Are you still serving breakfast?"

She smiles at me. "Breakfast usually ends at ten thirty, but I think we have some leftover doughnuts."

"That would be great. Thank you."

The woman scurries into the back and pulls out a basket of doughnuts.

"Thank you," I say again as I take a couple out of the basket.

"Are there any places in this area that you recommend I see while I'm here?"

She smiles. "Well, just walking around the city of Galway is beautiful. I'd recommend seeing the nearby castle and cathedral along with the Spanish Arch. I would also stop in a jeweler and get a Claddagh ring, especially if you are here with a special someone. And if you haven't made it to the Cliffs of Moher yet, I highly recommend them."

"Thanks," I say.

I take my doughnuts with me and then head out of the bed-and-breakfast. I walk down the street to the main city block and begin walking, taking in all of my surroundings. The town is beautiful, just like she said. I instantly fall in love with the beautiful colors of the storefronts. The stores are quaint and small, compared to the large and bright casinos I'm used to in Las Vegas. It's so much calmer here. Everyone smiles and says hi to me here. No one is in a rush here. It's nice. The only problem is, Killian isn't here with me.

I spend the day exploring many of the places the woman suggested, including the beautiful cathedral and Spanish Arch. I go into several jewelers and admire all of their Claddagh rings. And, every few hours or so, I check back into the bed-and-breakfast to see if Killian has made it back. Each time, I come up empty until I am starting to worry that something might be wrong.

I head back to the bed-and-breakfast around dinner-time. I don't have any cash and am thankful to find a small dinner of tea and shepherd's pie is included. I fall in love with the tea that I sip on when Killian finally comes back.

I glare at him when he walks in.

"I'm sorry," he says when he walks over to me.

"I don't want to hear it."

"I'm sorry. My phone calls took a lot longer than expected, and I found out my cousin doesn't live here anymore."

I narrow my eyes. "Where does he live?"

He grimaces. "Dublin."

I shake my head in frustration.

"We can take a bus tonight if you want."

"No. I want to stay here. At least for a few more days."

I can tell Killian wants to argue with me, but he doesn't.

He leans down to kiss me, but I brush him away. I can't. I'm too angry with him for leaving me alone all day and for still not telling me the complete truth about why we are here. I thought today would be full of answers about why we flew around the world, but instead I got nothing but worry.

I yawn.

"Come on," he says. "Let me get you to bed."

I stand and follow him back to our bedroom. We walk inside in silence and then begin undressing, both preparing for bed without speaking. I just take my jeans off, and climb into bed.

"I still have lots of questions," I say to Killian.

He removes his shirt, revealing his body that I immediately want to jump. I bite my lip and look away while he continues to undress. I will not fuck him, not after leaving me alone to worry. Not after lying to me time and time again.

"And I want to hear all of them."

I look at him, and my eyes brighten a little. He begins climbing into bed when his phone vibrates on the nightstand next to the bed, stopping him. He looks at the number and then to me, but I already know what he is going to say.

"I have to take this."

I feel him climbing back out of bed, and he puts his jeans back on. I close my eyes and roll over as he walks out the door. A single tear rolls down my cheek. I don't understand how I'm here with Killian, but have never felt more alone.

How did forty-eight hours change the course of our relation-

ship so severely? How is it possible to feel so distant from someone I thought I loved?

If this is the real Killian, I'm afraid I made a terrible mistake. I want the man who stood up for me in the courtroom. The man who couldn't keep his hands off me in the bedroom. Not the man whose work and own needs come before me.

27

KILLIAN

I watch Kinsley sleep. Her lips are pursed, and her now short locks curl around her flushed cheeks. I watch her chest rise and fall in a steady rhythm. I want to kiss her, but I don't think she would like that, not after leaving her alone and not telling her the truth of why we are here.

I didn't plan to spend the day away from her. It just happened. To contact the FBI without them tracking me, I had to go route the call through different locations, which required a computer and internet access that I didn't have at the bed-and-breakfast. I had to drive an hour away to get a laptop, and then I spent most of the day in various cafes using their internet.

I spent the whole day getting my ass chewed out by the FBI, but I think I finally convinced them that I did the only thing I could. The only problem is, they couldn't identify any criminals in the Felton Grand casino, which means the men don't have a record. And it means, we will be here for quite a while as they try to figure out who the men are that I overheard in Mexico and then again in the Felton Grand.

It also took me much longer to track down my cousin

whom I haven't seen in twenty years. It required me getting ahold of my father since he was the only one who knew my cousin's address. He finally gave me the address, which I guess was progress since the last time I saw him.

Today though can't be about the FBI or my cousin. Today has to be about fixing things with Kinsley. Since I told her in the alleyway that we had to leave the country, I have felt her slipping further and further away. I have felt the distance between us grow instead of us getting closer and closer together. And I can't stand to be growing apart when I have nothing left in my life, except for her.

She stirs, and her mouth opens in a cute yawn as her arms stretch over her head.

"Wake up, princess. It's a big day today."

Her eyes pop open and immediately glare at me.

"Why? Are you planning on leaving me again today?"

I smile at her feistiness. "No. I don't plan on leaving your sight today. Not for a second. Even when you have to go to the bathroom, I'm going to be there."

"Ew, I think that is taking it too far."

But she is smiling, which was the point.

"So, what are your big plans for today?" she asks.

"Well, since you explored the town, I thought I would take you to my favorite place in the world today."

Her eyes light up. "And where is that?"

"The Cliffs of Moher."

She firmly kisses me on the lips, but then she quickly pulls away when she realizes that she isn't really ready to be happy with me. Or at least she's not ready to show me she is happy with me again, but I'll take what I can get.

"I had our clothes laundered, but if we find a place, we should pick up some new clothes tonight or tomorrow."

"Thanks."

"Go get your cute butt dressed. I'll get dressed and call a cab to take us. I think it's about an hour away from here."

"Sounds good."

I watch her roll out of bed and walk in just a T-shirt to the bathroom. I can't keep my eyes off her bare legs as she walks. I'm desperate to have her. I'm desperate to feel close to her again. But I guess I'll just have to wait.

"Thanks," I say to the cab driver.

I hand him money for the fare and then climb out of the taxi. Kinsley follows me. We haven't spoken much today. Instead, we've just focused on being content with sitting next to each other. But I know her questions are coming, and I try to prepare myself for them as best as I can.

I take her hand and walk her to the edge of the cliffs. She doesn't speak as she takes in the awe-inspiring view, but I can see the amazement on her face. Her hand goes over her mouth to cover her shocked expression. Her eyes slowly shift left and right, trying to take every drop of beauty in. I let out a breath I didn't realize I had been holding when I see that she loves this place as much as I do.

I guide her to my favorite peaceful spot, and we sit so our legs dangle over the edge. I wrap my arm around her waist, and we just sit. We sit in the amazement of this place, and that alone makes me feel closer to her.

"Were you born or raised in Ireland?"

"No. I was born in Kansas, but my family is from Ireland. The only person left who lives here is my cousin. Every year, up until I was in high school, we would save up money to come back here for two or three weeks."

"It's magical here."

I nod. "This is my favorite place in Ireland. I could spend all day here, just sitting and looking out at the blue water and the cliffs."

"Me, too."

And that's exactly what we do for an hour. We just sit in peace.

"What do you imagine for our future?" she asks.

I curiously look at her. Of all the questions that I know are burning inside her, that is what she asks. I try to answer but then stop because it's the one question I have no idea how to answer.

"Me, too," she says, smiling at my non-answer and turning to look back at the water. "I have no idea, and when I'm sitting in a place like this that makes me feel so small, it makes me feel like whatever I choose to do with my life, whatever we choose to do together, it's not big enough to matter. It's not big enough to make an impact on the world."

I reach up and tuck her breeze blown hair behind her ear. I rub my thumb across her cheek. "You are big enough to matter to me. And, as for our future together, I don't know, but I do know my future will always involve you in some capacity or another. I can't imagine a life without you."

She nods, satisfied with my answer.

"What made you decide to become an FBI agent?"

I stare off into the distance. "It's a long story."

"I want to hear it."

I turn to face her to show her how hard it is for me to tell her this, the worst mistake of my life. But when she looks back at me with such hope and purity in her eyes, it gives me the courage to tell her. After all, I know her worst mistake. She should know mine.

"I grew up in Marysville, Kansas. A tiny little town in the

middle of nowhere. It was just the four of us living in a modest house. My mother worked as a nurse. My father ran the only hotel in the town. So, most of the time, at home, it was just me and my older brother."

She smiles. "I didn't know you had a brother. I always wished I had a sibling."

I nod. "Kieran, my brother, was the best. He was seven years older than me, but he was never ashamed of me. He was always protecting me. My name was Liam up until I was six or seven. I was an awkward child who got made fun of a lot. Lame Liam was practically my nickname.

"When Kieran found out, he started calling me by my middle name Killian. He said that it sounded like kill 'em, and he thought it fit me better since I was so tough. It stuck, and that has been my name ever since."

Kinsley looks at me with concern in her eyes. "You said your brother *was* the best."

I nod. "When I was seventeen, I was a bit of a wild child. By then, Kieran had been away from Marysville for several years while I was stuck alone in the town. I was girl crazy. I was bored. I was unfocused. I started smoking marijuana and skipping school."

She looks at me intently, listening to my every word.

"One day, me and Summer were hanging out after school, smoking marijuana and bored out of our minds in the cornfields."

"Summer?"

"She was the girl I wanted."

I see Kinsley grimace when I say Summer was *the girl*.

"I mean, I was seventeen, so I was attracted to any woman who gave me any attention."

She smiles. "Continue your story."

"Anyway, my dumbass was restless and trying to impress

Summer. Kieran was working for the FBI. That was always his dream. He was always so focused. He always had such a clear idea of what his goals were while I was clueless and wild.

"That night, I got the idea to go find him. So, I drove Summer in my pickup truck from Marysville, Kansas, to Chicago, where he was working undercover. We drove all night, but when we got to Chicago we had no idea where Kieran was. So, I called him. Told him we needed somewhere to stay."

She nods while biting her lip in the cute way she does.

"Kieran came, of course, but by then, we weren't in the best part of town. I was looking to show Summer a good time, and my stupid young self thought we could score some good party drugs while we were in Chicago. The people we were buying from just so happened to be some of the people Kieran was investigating. He showed up; I blew his cover. I joked with the drug dealers that he worked for the FBI, but not to worry he was my brother. We were cool. The men opened fire."

Tears sting in my eyes, but I have to continue. I have to tell her. I have to show her one little part of my world that I can tell her. "The image of my brother, the person who cared about me most, getting shot in the heart is an image that haunts me every day of my life. He was shot twice in the chest because I blew his cover. The guys shot at me and Summer, but they quickly took off when sirens sounded in the distance."

I remember running over to him and pressing my hands to his blood-soaked chest. I tried to stop the bleeding, but there was just...just so much blood. It was impossible to stop. I remember just telling him to hang on, to just hang on, but of course, he was already dead.

"I got my own brother killed."

Kinsley wraps her arms around me and holds me while we cry together in his favorite spot that later became my favorite spot. She doesn't try to tell me that it wasn't my fault because it was my fault. She just shares in my pain with me as tears fall down both of our faces.

"So, that's why you became an FBI agent? For him?" she asks when she is able to speak through her tears.

I nod when my tears run dry. And then she kisses me on the lips, so softly and so carefully, like she thinks she will break me if she kisses me harder.

"You can kiss me. I won't break."

She smiles. "I'm afraid if I kiss you harder, we won't make it back to the bed-and-breakfast before things get out of hand, and we get arrested for public indecency."

I press my lips hard against hers and slip my tongue into her mouth until she's moaning crazily against my lips. She pushes me away though before I can get her really riled up. She bites her gorgeous lip that I want back in my mouth.

The skies open now, as it almost always does in Ireland, and little droplets of rain begin pelting down on top of us.

"Thank you," Kinsley says through the rain.

"For what?"

"For telling me a truth."

I smile and kiss her again until the rain is beginning to soak through our clothes. Even then, I don't want to pull away because I've never felt so connected to someone in my life.

"We should head back."

She looks at me, reluctant to get up, but she shivers. So, I put my arm around her, and we walk back to catch a cab to the bed-and-breakfast.

28

KINSLEY

I'M STILL SHIVERING from the wet cold rain when we make it back to our room in the bed-and-breakfast.

Killian lets go of me and walks to the bathroom. I hear him turn the water on in the shower, and I walk in.

"It should be warm soon. I laid out a towel for you as well. Are you hungry? I can go get us some food while you are showering," Killian says.

I shake my head at this incredible man. A man who is so selfless that he chose a career based on the love he had for his brother. The guilt of thinking he's the reason his brother is dead is overwhelming him. I understand that feeling.

"I'm not hungry."

He nods. "I'll let you enjoy your shower then."

He starts to walk past me, but I place my hand against his chest, stopping him. He raises one eyebrow at me. I grab the hem of his shirt and lift it over his head. I place my hand on his bare chest to feel his heart beating rapidly, matching my own heartbeat.

"Join me."

A wicked grin forms on his face.

He peels my shirt, and then my pants, off of me. His appreciative gaze travels over my body, warming me with just his look. Suddenly, I'm not cold anymore. I unhook my bra and slip out of my panties, and his gaze somehow intensifies.

I smile and then step under the warm shower. I crook my finger, indicating for him to join me. He doesn't even wait to remove his jeans. He just steps into the shower with me, making me laugh. I quickly push his jeans down because I can't stand not to feel completely lost in him any longer. I need our bodies connected after such an emotional day. I might not have gotten any answers about why we traveled halfway across the world, but I don't really care anymore. I got so much more than answers. I got his feelings. I got one little piece of his soul, and that piece is more than enough to keep me sane until I find out more.

Killian reaches behind me and grabs a bar of soap. He begins running the soap over my shoulders, washing me. He moves slowly down each of my arms, sending shivers all over my body. He notices and presses his body against me as he continues to wash me. He slowly washes my breasts in circles. He moves the bar down my stomach and then between my legs.

I let out a gasp at his touch. And then he is moving down each of my legs, making sure to wash every inch of me. When he is finished washing me, he spins me around so my back is to him. He grabs my arms and moves them until I'm holding on to the wall of the shower, and his cock is pressing against my ass.

"I need you, princess."

His cock presses at my wet entrance.

"I'm yours."

He finds a condom in his jeans that are still in the floor

of the shower, puts it on, and then he gently pushes inside me, slowly stretching me, taking his time, like he never has before. I can feel every inch of him as he moves further and further inside me until I gasp when he stretches me fully. One of his hands grabs my breast while the other moves liquid around my clit. His touches are slow and deliberate and emotional.

I feel the water falling down my face, and I'm taken back to the cliffs we were just on. Killian thrusts into me, but each thrust isn't about sexual need; it's all pure emotion. Each thrust is Killian giving a little of himself to me. Each touch is him sharing his pain and love until I'm feeling everything he is feeling, the love and the pain, until I'm not sure which one is a stronger emotion.

"I love you," he whispers against my ear.

"I love you, too."

But this, whatever we are making, is more than love. It's trust.

Killian moves faster, and I match his rhythm until we are coming together, each screaming the other's name, connected in a way we have never been before. We're connected in a way that can never be broken.

Killian hesitantly turns the water off and slides out of me. His moves are slow, as if he's afraid the connection will be broken, but nothing can break the connection we just had.

I step out of the shower and begin to dry off. I hand him a towel, which he wraps around his waist before wrapping his arms around me.

He stares at us in the mirror. "God, I could take you again right now."

I laugh. "I know. I feel the same way, like I can never get enough of you."

He nods. "We should at least try. All night if we have to."

I bite my lip. "Okay, but first, we should eat. Then, we should do that again and again."

I watch him walk out of the bathroom. I finish drying off and then meet him in the bedroom. He's already dressed when I get there. I walk over to grab my clothes out of the bag, but he puts a hand on my arm, stopping me.

"Don't get dressed."

"How will we go get food if I don't get dressed?"

"I want you to stay here, naked. I saw a pizza place across the street. I'll bring back some pizzas."

I smile.

"You stay naked. I'll be right back." He leans over and softly kisses me on the lips, and then he leaves me alone in our room.

I sigh, not sure about what I should do now. I walk back to the bathroom and gather our wet clothes. I take them back to the small closet and begin hanging them to dry. We really need to get more clothes tomorrow. I hang up Killian's jacket, but it keeps falling off the hanger. I pick it up again, and that's when I feel something stiff in the pocket. I reach my hand into the pocket and pull out a note and an envelope that I assume contains some cash. I read the note quickly that Granddad wrote but learn nothing new other then he was saving his own skin.

I flip the envelope over and am shocked to see my name on it. I carry the envelope with me as I take a seat on the bed. I don't know what this envelope contains, but whatever it is, it is something Killian was hiding from me. It's the same feeling I got when I opened Tristan's bag of cocaine.

I shiver and decide to climb under the covers, but the covers don't stop my shivers. My shivers won't stop until I open the envelope, so with shaking hands, I do. I open the envelope and pull out the thick piece of paper it contains. I unfold it until it's a flat piece of paper.

Then, I look at the handwritten words my father wrote me. I read word after word. My eyes skim faster than my mind can even read. This is what Killian was keeping from me. In this one piece of paper, I learn everything I need to know about my grandfather, my father, and even Killian.

My body shakes, and my cheeks turn red. I was wrong when I thought the connection Killian and I shared couldn't be broken. It was just broken with one lie and one secret.

I fold the paper back up and put it back in the envelope. I turn off the lights before I climb back into bed just before I hear Killian fumbling at the door. I close my eyes and pretend to sleep as Killian walks in and flicks on the lights.

I hear him walk over to me.

"Princess," he says, kissing my cheek.

"Mmhmm," I moan but keep my eyes closed.

"You should eat."

"Too sleepy," I moan.

He sighs. I hear him take off his clothes. The lights flicker back off, and then he climbs into bed. His arms go around me, and somehow, that motion still relaxes me, even after knowing that he lied to me.

"Sleep sounds good." He softly kisses me on the neck. "We can eat and fuck later."

I pull his arms around me tighter.

"When I was getting the food though, I thought about what you asked me earlier. About what I see for our future. When I was standing in line, they were selling these little Claddagh rings that represent love, loyalty, and friendship. I realized then what I wanted. You. Just you. I want to be married to you. I want to have those kids you told me you wanted. Nothing else matters."

I try to keep my breathing normal as a tear falls down my cheek.

"I know it's too soon to be thinking like that. And I'm not going to officially ask you to marry me. Not until we have a lot more answers, but I just wanted you to know that. I see my future, and I'm married to you. What do you think? Could you see yourself married to me someday after all of this is over? Would you marry me if things were different?"

"Maybe."

I feel his lips curl up into a smile. "I'll take that as a yes."

He holds me tighter, and then his breathing slows as he drifts to sleep.

But more tears fall down my cheeks. Because that *maybe* doesn't mean yes. That *maybe* wasn't me hesitating to answer him. It was me deceiving him. Because a future where we are married and living happily ever after will never happen.

29

KILLIAN

I wake up and reach across to touch Kinsley after not having her again like we talked about last night. I'm feeling desperate to have her, but my hand comes up empty. I sit up and look around the room, but I don't see her. I get out of bed and check the bathroom, but she isn't in there either. If she went exploring again without me, I'm going to kill her. She doesn't understand that it's just not safe for her to go out by herself.

I walk back to the bedroom to put clothes on to go find her. When I see a note written on a napkin lying next to the bed, I pick it up to read it.

Maybe...never. I read my father's letter that you hid from me. I'm sorry, but I can't be with you. I can't be with someone that lies and hides so many things from me. I'm going home. I'll face whatever charges the FBI have for me, but I'm done running. I'm sorry that I no longer love you. I hope you can find happiness with the FBI.

—Kinsley

"Fuck!" I scream when I finish reading the note. "Fuck! Fuck! Fuck!"

I crumble the napkin and throw it onto the floor. I grab my clothes and quickly put them on. Then, I run out the door and out onto the street. I have to find her. I don't know what the hell she is doing.

How can she not love me anymore when I was inside her last night? How can love disappear so quickly?

I run a block down the street before I realize this is useless. She's not just wandering down the main street of Galway.

I run back to the bed-and-breakfast. I ring the damn little bell at the entrance and wait for the owner to come downstairs.

"The lady I was traveling with, have you seen her this morning?"

The owner looks at me for a second. "Yes, she was down rather early, around six. I hadn't even put breakfast out yet, and she was already out the door. I figured she had an early sightseeing day."

"Thanks," I say before running up the stairs to our bedroom.

I look through the bag and find most of the money along with her passport are gone. "Fuck!"

I go to the closet and grab my jacket. I feel inside and find that the envelope her dad wrote her and the note her grandfather wrote is gone. She really did find it. She knows the truth. And she is turning herself into the FBI because of it. She just doesn't realize that going home isn't safe either. The men that were working with her father and grandfather are dangerous and they are in Las Vegas. They will kill her. The FBI won't be able to protect her.

I pace back and forth in the room. I pick the napkin off the floor and reread it, but none of it makes any more sense than the first time I read it. I'm still just as lost as I was before. The only thing I can read from the note is that she doesn't care about me anymore. She doesn't love me.

So, instead, I do the only thing I can do. I take my cell phone out of my pocket, and I call Agent Hayes.

"Byrne?"

"Hayes, I need…"

"You are in a lot of trouble Byrne. Bisson is furious. Just tell us where you are. Come home and then we can straighten everything out. There is a protocol you have to follow if you think a witness is in danger. This isn't it. If she really is in danger she should be in witness protection."

"I know Hayes. I just couldn't leave her with you. I don't trust anyone but myself right now. But listen! I need you to see if a Megan Slade or Erin Buffet has booked any flights out of Ireland today. And then I need you to assemble a team to pick her up if she did."

"What is happening?"

"I think Kinsley is turning herself in to the FBI. I think she's had enough of the running."

"What?"

"I'm going after her. Just tell me where she is headed, and I'll be on a flight to go after her. Can you do that for me?"

"Yes. I'll text you."

I grab a cab to the Dublin Airport, and I'm an hour away before Agent Hayes texts me, saying that she's on a flight to New York and then has a connecting flight to Las Vegas. I text back, saying I'm taking the next flight and I will be wherever she is going soon. I just hope that we get to her before her grandfather's men. She's turning herself in to the FBI, but that won't stop his men from trying to get to her first. She's in danger, and I have to protect her. I promised I would.

———

The flight to New York takes forever, and it feels longer than forever when I don't know what the hell is going on. I run off the flight and am surprised to find Agent Hayes standing just inside the terminal. I figured he would have been with Kinsley.

"Did you get her?"

"No."

"No? Why the hell not?"

"Killian Byrne, you are under arrest," a man says from behind me.

Then, I'm surrounded by agents who grab ahold of me, and handcuffs go around my wrist.

"I'm sorry," Agent Hayes says.

Then, he walks away, leaving me to be arrested.

I'm sorry, too. I'm sorry I failed to protect Kinsley Felton. I failed her father. I failed Kinsley. I failed the FBI. And I failed myself. And I don't know who else is going to have to pay for that mistake.

And, now that I'm being arrested, I won't even have a chance to fix my mistake.

30

KINSLEY

I WIPE a tear from my eye at the thought of never seeing Killian again. I hate that I broke his heart, but it was the only way to protect him. What I hate worse is that I lied to him, I'm not going to turn myself in. I'm doing the only thing I can do after reading my father's letter. I'm making things right and fixing my family's mistakes.

"Boarding group three can now board," the gate agent says over the speakers.

I stand from the blue seat I'm sitting on in the terminal with my plane ticket and bag in hand. I wait in a short line until I reach the gate agent. I hand her my ticket, which she scans, and then hands back.

"Have a good flight to Cancún," she says.

I nod and force my legs to move forward. I force my body to move toward what has been my destiny all along. I force my legs to board a plane to Mexico.

The End

Thank you for reading Maybe Never! Want to read more of

Kinsley & Killian's story? Find out what happens next here>>>Maybe Always

Sign up to get notified when my new books release and get a FREE ebook here>>>EllaMiles.com/freebooks

Want to order signed paperbacks? Visit: store.ellamiles.com

MAYBE ALWAYS PREVIEW

"MA'AM, CAN I get you anything to drink?" the stewardess says.

I open my eyes and then immediately yawn. I've been flying for over twenty-four hours with minimal sleep.

"Coffee," I say. I have only about an hour left in this last flight. I need to start waking up.

"Here you go," she says, handing me the coffee.

I take it and set the cup on the tray table in front of me that also has my new passport and the letter my father wrote to me.

I flip the passport open again and read the name Hannah Grove. I got the passport from the same abandoned building Killian got our previous fake ones from in Tokyo. It was risky. I didn't know if Killian or the FBI would check there. Even if they do, I paid the man almost ten times the amount the FBI usually does to ensure loyalty to me and not them. They can't know where I am or where I'm going. Although I know they will figure it out soon.

I told Killian I was going to turn myself in. When I got to

the airport, I called the FBI and told them the same. I even bought a direct flight from Dublin to New York.

I just didn't get on it.

I'd learned from Killian that the best way not to be found was to get good and lost. Change passports. Change planes. So, that's what I did.

I'm not going to turn myself in. I'm going to Mexico. I'm going to end this. I'm not going to let Killian get hurt for my family. I'm not going to let him lose his job for me. I love him, and I know he loves me, but he can't keep harboring a fugitive. He can't keep protecting me and keep the job that is so important to him. I just hope the FBI will believe that Killian is loyal to them and not me.

I shake my head, thinking back to my conversation with Agent Hayes.

"Hello, this is Agent Hayes."

I nervously hold the pay phone in my hand and take a deep breath. I have to tell him. I have to do this.

"This is Kinsley Felton."

Agent Hayes sucks in a breath on the other end of the phone, but his voice is calm when he speaks, "Where are you?"

"I can't tell you that. All you need to know is that I'm buying a flight back home. My flight gets in at eight tomorrow morning at LaGuardia Airport and then I have a connection to Las Vegas at nine. I'll cooperate. I'll do whatever you want."

"Is Agent Byrne with you?"

"No. He's been tracking me. I saw him in London, but he didn't find me. He's the reason I'm turning myself in. I can't keep living my life, running from the law."

"That's good, Kinsley. Just get on that flight, we will meet you in New York and fly back with you to Las Vegas. Then we can talk. You aren't in any trouble. We just want to talk."

I know he is lying. He doesn't just want to talk. He wants to arrest me and my grandfather. If only he knew how much bigger this is than just money laundering and tax evasion. It's much bigger. And I'm the only one who can put a stop to it.

"I'll be on the flight," I say.

I sip on my coffee. I don't know if Killian has a chance at staying in the FBI's good graces, but at least he will be safe in the US and not here, trying to protect me. No one can protect me. As much as my father thought he could, no one can. My family is too involved. And, as much as I want to just abandon my family, I need to make things right. After I figure it out, then I can save Killian's career by making him seem like the hero.

I unfold the letter my father wrote and begin reading it for the hundredth time.

My dearest princess,

If you are reading this, I am no longer with you, and I'm so sorry about that. There is nothing more I wanted than to spend forever with you, protecting you from what I now must tell you. I need you to know that, even when you read the last word on this page, I love you, princess. I love you more than everything else in my life even if I wasn't always able to show you.

I don't know how to tell you this, but I have to. I'm not a good person. Your grandfather is worse. Your great-grandfather might have been worse than him. We aren't casino and hotel owners. Not at our hearts. We are criminals. We like greed and money above everything and will do anything to keep it.

By now, you might have found out that we are money launderers. We don't pay our fair share of taxes. We have lied and cheated our investors out of money. And, while that is all true, it was just a cover for what we are really involved in.

I can't believe I'm even going to tell you the worst of it because you will never forgive me after I do. You will hate me, and your hatred for me will be valid. I won't be there to defend myself, but you deserve to know who your family is. You deserve to know the truth.

So, here it is. We are smugglers. It started off small. Drugs and guns in small amounts, but it quickly grew. We realized we could make more money doing that than we ever could running hotels and casinos. Then, we found reinvesting the money into our casinos and hotels would make us even more money and keep our real activities hidden.

But the smuggling of drugs and guns soon grew large, so large that we got even greedier. We wanted more. Always more and more. We never had enough.

So, we grew to smuggling jewels, diamonds, anything of value. And that satisfied us for a while until we found out what our partners really wanted, what they would pay top dollar for.

People.

They wanted us to smuggle people.

Our immediate response should have been no, but we couldn't say no because we were in too deep with these people. And, to be honest, we didn't want to tell them no. We wanted the money and excitement that came with smuggling. So, it made no difference to us if we were smuggling drugs, guns, diamonds, or people. They were all the same to us.

I realize now that it was a mistake. But, at the time, it was just our next adventure, an adventure we passed down from generation to generation. From son to son.

I didn't realize how wrong it was until I had you, and then my world changed. At first, I thought I could pass the company to you along with all of our illegal activities, but we quickly realized that wouldn't be a possibility. You were too delicate to take over. You would have ruined everything we worked so hard to build.

So, instead, we thought we could pass it on to your husband. But we would have to choose your husband very carefully to ensure we could pass the company on to him.

Finding you a husband became our new mission. Tristan was horrible. We knew he was a druggie and couldn't be trusted around drugs, so we set him up. Of course, that turned into a mess when you were caught with the drugs instead of him. But, in the end, it all worked out. He was gone from your life, and you gave us the deciding power to choose your next boyfriend and who your husband would be. It couldn't have worked out better.

We let you date Eli because he was harmless, but we knew he would never work out.

And then I met Killian. Killian was perfect. Strong, decisive, and loyal. He would do anything I asked of him without a second thought. And I asked a lot of him.

He was strong enough to run the company and keep up with the illegal activities while still keeping you protected from them.

We thought we had found the perfect solution.

Except we hadn't. I found out he was FBI. I was going to have to kill him, a man I had grown to love as a son. I was going to have to shoot him in cold blood.

Now, you need to know I've killed before, so it wouldn't have been an unusual thing for me to do, but I've never killed someone I thought would one day be my family, someone my daughter would someday marry.

But I had no other choice. The day came when I had to kill him. I had the gun. I had Killian alone, but I couldn't do it. I couldn't kill him, but if I didn't, we were all as good as dead. You were as good as dead. I couldn't have that.

I had to protect you. That became my obsession. I would do anything to protect you.

So, I made the decision to sacrifice myself and your grandfa-ther to keep you safe. I told Killian I would give him everything he needed to put us away in prison if he promised to keep you safe. He promised, and I believe him. Killian will keep his promise and keep you safe.

I haven't told him everything yet, but I will. All he knows about is the money laundering. He's gained my trust though, so I can now tell him the rest. Now, I can tell him everything, and he can help me nail these guys, but it will be at the cost of me and your grandfather going to jail. We deserve it though. And I would do it all again to keep you safe.

But, if for some reason I die before I get a chance to tell Killian everything, you have to tell him. You have to give him this letter. You have to let him protect you. Promise me, princess, that you will be safe. Your safety is the only thing that matters to me.

I included the address to our main smuggling facility in Mexico at the bottom of this letter. I've already laid the ground-work to make sure Killian will be accepted as my successor. He will be able to gain access, and then he can call in the FBI to arrest everyone that is involved in the smuggling.

I'm so sorry, princess. I hope that you can forgive me some-day, but I don't know if you will be able to. I'm sorry, but you will be safe.

All my love,
   Dad

I wipe away a tear. I cry each time I read the damn letter.

I didn't even know my father. I knew nothing about him at all. He wasn't a nice, caring father. He was a criminal who ruined who knows how many people's lives.

If he thought I was going to just let Killian come in and fix all my family's problems, he was wrong. There is no way

I'm going to let the man I love risk his life to protect me. Not when I know there is a real chance Killian could be killed if he tried to arrest any of these men. I can't let him die while protecting me even if it is his job as an FBI agent. I won't let him do that. Not on my account. Not when his cover has been blown.

No, I have to find a way to infiltrate them myself. Once I have evidence that we really do smuggle people, then I can call in reinforcements to arrest everyone.

I fold the letter back up and put it in my pocket. I put the tray table up and sit in silence as the plane lands before I go through the long process of exiting the plane and going through customs. Then, I'll be off to form a plan in a nice hotel; the last nice hotel I might ever stay in.

If only I could find a way to contact my grandfather, then I could easily put an end to this, but I don't even know if he will be in Cancún when I land.

I don't have a choice though. Even if he isn't there, I have to go to the address my father provided. And, when I do, I will be the criminal. Despite my good intentions, there will be no distinction with the law. The FBI will arrest me if I make it out of there alive. And being with Killian will no longer be a possibility. But at least he will be safe and be free to continue working as an FBI agent while I pay for my family's sins.

Find out what happens next here>>>Maybe Always

FREE BOOKS

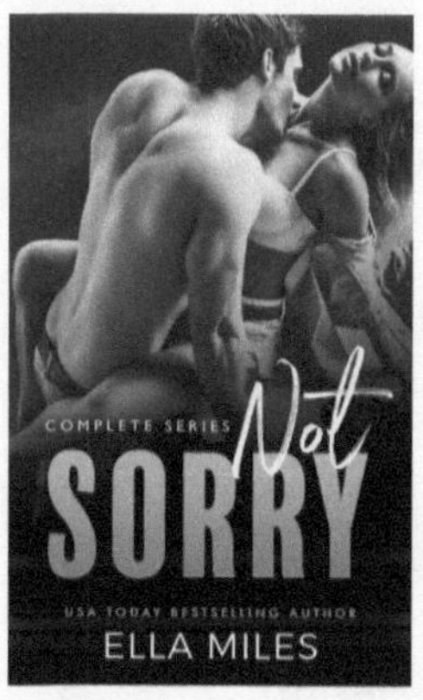

Read **Not Sorry** for **FREE!** And sign up to get my latest releases, updates, and more goodies here→EllaMiles.com/freebooks

Follow me on BookBub to get notified of my new releases and recommendations here→Follow on BookBub Here

Join Ella's Bellas FB group for giveaways and FUN→Join Ella's Bellas Here

ALSO BY ELLA MILES

MAYBE, DEFINITELY SERIES:

Maybe Yes

Maybe Never

Maybe Always

Definitely Yes

Definitely No

Definitely Forever

Truth or Lies (Coming 2019):

Taken by Lies

Betrayed by Truths

Trapped by Lies

Stolen by Truths

Possessed by Lies

Consumed by Truths

DIRTY SERIES:

Dirty Beginning

Dirty Obsession

Dirty Addiction

Dirty Revenge

ALIGNED SERIES:

Aligned: Volume 1 (Free Series Starter)

Aligned: Volume 2

Aligned: Volume 3

Aligned: Volume 4

Aligned: The Complete Series Boxset

UNFORGIVABLE SERIES:

Heart of a Thief

Heart of a Liar

Heart of a Prick

Unforgivable: The Complete Series Boxset

STANDALONES:

Pretend I'm Yours

Finding Perfect

Savage Love

Too Much

Not Sorry

ABOUT THE AUTHOR

Ella Miles writes steamy romance, including everything from dark suspense romance that will leave you on the edge of your seat to contemporary romance that will leave you laughing out loud or crying. Most importantly, she wants you to feel everything her characters feel as you read.

Ella is currently living her own happily ever after near the Rocky Mountains with her high school sweetheart husband. Her heart is also taken by her goofy five year old black lab who is scared of everything, including her own shadow.

Ella is a USA Today Bestselling Author & Top 50 Bestselling Author.

Stalk Ella at:
www.ellamiles.com
ella@ellamiles.com